TELL ME I'M WRONG

ADAM CROFT

First published in Great Britain in 2018.

This edition published in 2021 by Black Cannon Publishing.

ISBN: 978-1-912599-56-1

A CIP catalogue record for this book is available from the British Library.

Printed and bound in Great Britain by Clays Ltd, Elcograf S.p.A.

GET MORE OF MY BOOKS FREE!

To say thank you for buying this book, I'd like to invite you to my exclusive *VIP Club*, and give you some of my books and short stories for FREE.

To join the club, head to adamcroft.net/vip-club **and two free books will be sent to you straight away! And the best thing is it won't cost you a penny — ever.**

Adam Croft

For more information, visit my website: adamcroft.net

MORE BOOKS BY ADAM CROFT

RUTLAND CRIME SERIES

1. What Lies Beneath
2. On Borrowed Time
3. In Cold Blood

KNIGHT & CULVERHOUSE CRIME THRILLERS

1. Too Close for Comfort
2. Guilty as Sin
3. Jack Be Nimble
4. Rough Justice
5. In Too Deep
6. In The Name of the Father
7. With A Vengeance
8. Dead & Buried
9. In Too Deep
10. Snakes & Ladders

PSYCHOLOGICAL THRILLERS

- Her Last Tomorrow

- Only The Truth
- In Her Image
- Tell Me I'm Wrong
- The Perfect Lie
- Closer To You

KEMPSTON HARDWICK MYSTERIES

1. Exit Stage Left
2. The Westerlea House Mystery
3. Death Under the Sun
4. The Thirteenth Room
5. The Wrong Man

All titles are available to order from all good book shops.

Signed and personalised books available at adamcroft.net/shop

EBOOK-ONLY SHORT STORIES

- Gone
- The Harder They Fall
- Love You To Death
- The Defender

To find out more, visit adamcroft.net

For Julian

ONE

Riley Markham wiped the snot from under his nose as he watched the football bobble along the rutted ground towards his friends.

'You out tomorrow?' one of them called to him, kicking the ball back.

'Might be. Have to ask Mum,' he said, walking away, the football now under his arm.

Mum would let him. She always let him. He'd often heard her telling Dad that it was better than having him sitting around playing computer games all day. Mum liked her peace and quiet, working from home. And Riley liked playing football with his friends.

He was getting quite good at it now. He'd been playing football in the garden with Dad since he was two. He was rubbish at first. But he'd been playing every chance he got in the five years since then, and he knew it wouldn't be long before one of the scouts came calling.

Maybe Arsenal or Manchester United. That would make him *really* famous, but secretly he'd quite like to play for Crystal Palace. He really liked their kit.

It had been hot today. It was always hot at this time of year. That was why he loved the summer holidays. That and not having to go to school, obviously.

He tried to remember what Mum said was for dinner tonight. He'd be back in plenty of time so it wouldn't really matter. Fish fingers, he thought. Something like that. Afterwards they'd watch some telly, then he'd go to bed. Mum and Dad let him stay up until eight now. Then all the boring grown-up programmes started, like *Holby City*.

It wasn't far from the field to his house. Nothing was far in the village. That was the best thing about it. Except when they had to get something that you couldn't get in the village, which was quite a lot. Then they'd have to drive out, which would take *ages* because the village was miles from anywhere. But Mum and Dad liked it because it was safe. By that, they meant it was *so* far away from anything that the bad guys just didn't bother coming here.

Riley didn't like bad guys. No-one liked bad guys. Everyone liked the good guys, like Superman and Scooby Doo. They would never do bad stuff.

All the kids round here played in the field. It was great. They could play football, hide in the bushes or just ride their bikes around. The houses were all pretty nearby. Riley's was, anyway. He had to walk back past the stream, over the footbridge and in through the back gate. 'Keep on the fence side, away from the water,' Mum would always say. Riley thought this was daft, because the water wasn't very deep anyway. It probably wouldn't go past his ankles. Definitely not past his knees. Unless it rained, and then it was deeper. Sometimes people's gardens would flood. Riley thought that was great, because it all looked like a swamp where monsters might live. But he wasn't allowed down that way when it flooded, which was rubbish.

The ground was really dry at the moment, because it had been hot for a few days. Riley could see it starting to crack in some places, and he imagined it cracking more and more, until the whole ground opened up and revealed a huge underground cave. That would be great. He could go down and explore it, or keep it to himself so no-one else knew it was there. It could be his secret den.

It was almost ten minutes after leaving his friends, and he would be home soon. There was a little bridge over the stream a little further up, then he'd walk through the foot-path and up the road to his house.

He almost didn't see the person in front of him. He saw the shoes first, then quickly looked up and saw the familiar face.

'Oh, hi.'

'Hello,' came the response.

It didn't quite seem right. They didn't say anything else. Just looked at him. To get past, Riley would have to walk closer to the water — something his mum never liked him doing — but he didn't have a choice. This was getting silly. He stepped to the side and went to carry on walking, but the arm around his waist pulled him backwards and upwards, the other hand clamping across his mouth as the person dragged him off into the bushes.

He wanted to scream, but couldn't. The person had clamped their big hand right across his nose and mouth and he was struggling to breathe.

He felt himself get winded, the air rushing out of him as he landed flat on his back on the hard ground, the prickly bush digging into his arms and head. He could feel the sensation of blood trickling down from his head — something he'd not felt since he cracked his head open falling off the swings a couple of years ago.

The arm that had been around his waist was now pressing down on his throat, crushing his windpipe and pushing all the life out of his young body.

A high-pitched whistling sound started in his ears and his vision started to go watery. Before long, black edges started to appear, and he was no longer able to fight.

Everything went black.

TWO

MEGAN

I close the front door and immediately feel a surge of panic and dread. Now I'm on my own until Chris comes home. Our parents have been great in helping to take some of the load off me, looking after Evie while I try to catch up on some much-needed sleep, but Chris's mum can't keep her all day and inevitably it's just the two of us alone again.

I don't believe babies as young as Evie should be babysat by other people, but there really is no other option. I was told new mothers tended to struggle a bit after the birth of a baby, but I didn't think it would be this bad.

We've never been able to bond properly. I went in with all the best intentions, but those very quickly went out the window. Evie wouldn't take to breastfeeding, no matter what I did. I wouldn't risk my child's health by using formula, so I've had to express and store it in bottles. It means she's getting all the nutrition she needs, but it definitely hasn't helped us bond.

They say the bond between a new mother and her baby is immediate and irreplaceable. I thought maybe my bond with Evie was just starting a bit later than usual, but six months on I still feel burdened as opposed to flowing with love.

I haven't told Chris any of this — not word for word — but he knows. It's affected our relationship too. He's been more distant, spending more and more time away from home. The school holidays usually meant we'd get to spend plenty of time together. We were delighted when we found out we were expecting. I had visions of us going out on walks and generally just spending more time together as a family.

As it turns out, none of that happened. He very quickly started going out on more fishing days and generally finding excuses not to be at home. He said he needed his space. He isn't getting any sleep or relaxation at home, but then again neither am I. That's what parenting's all about.

He's always liked his fishing, and I assumed it would be something he'd either try to maintain or would probably, inevitably, have to cut back on once Evie was born. Instead, it went the other way. He goes to a spot about two miles out of the village, where the stream opens up into the main river. He used to go at the weekends, getting up at the crack of dawn and coming back mid-morning to get his planning and marking done for the week. Now he's coming back later and later, often early in the evening.

It's amazing how all your plans and ideals can go out of the window so quickly. I had all these visions of a wonderful family unit, the three of us on days out together, smiling and laughing. How wrong I was.

I look at the clock on the mantelpiece. Four thirty. It'll probably be a good hour or so before Chris is even home.

I've got to admit it — he's good with Evie. The only problem is that he's never here. I know he's struggling too. He's finding it hard to come to terms not only with being a new parent, but dealing with what I'm going through. In the early days I was desperate to bond with Evie, yearning to create some sort of deep connection with her. Chris didn't even get a look in. Now I wonder whether it's my fault he's been so distant.

Evie's in her bouncer on the kitchen floor as I shovel handfuls of washing into the washing machine. That's one thing no-one tells you about having children. Despite the fact you've only added one tiny half-person to the family, somehow your washing loads quadruple in size.

The machine's ancient, and after each wash I need to drag it back across the room to where it's meant to be. The noise is horrendous too, so I take Evie out of the bouncer and jab the button on the front of the washing machine to get it started, before quickly closing the door and taking her through to the living room.

After a few moments, she's started fussing. I pick her up and hold her against me, trying to soothe her, as I go to grab a bottle of expressed milk from the fridge. As soon as I enter the kitchen she's wailing, the noise of the washing machine rattling around both of our heads. I close the door behind me again and go into the downstairs bathroom, running the hot tap and filling the sink with warm water, to bring the temperature of the milk bottle up.

'It's alright,' I say to her in the calmest voice I can muster. 'It's alright. It's just warming up. Won't be a minute.'

She coughs and splutters as she cries, and I have visions of having to change yet another top. More for the washing machine.

After a couple of minutes, the temperature of the milk is lukewarm and I bring the bottle through to the living room.

Evie feeds well. She always does just after she's been with George and Maggie. Part of me wonders whether they time it so that I'll have to do a feed after she's dropped back here. An attempt to help me bond with her. The thought is quite sweet, but it really isn't working. I hope to God it does, though. I hope to God it does. Because if it doesn't, I don't know what I'll do.

THREE

CHRIS

My walk home is taken up by thoughts. Always the thoughts. That's why I go fishing in the first place. Although I'm left alone with my mind, I'm far calmer. I tend to feel more peaceful.

There's never much to catch down there, but that's not the point. Sprats and tiddlers, mostly. Further downstream there's a lot more, but there's also a lot more people. Around the part I fish, there's no-one. No walkers, either. They tend to be around the village end, where it's more of a stream. I like the solitude. It's my escape. I've got my own little spot, where I'm quite happy to just sit and watch the sun move across the sky, occasionally feeling the slightest pull on my rod as I catch something.

I throw the fish straight back, provided they survive being reeled in. There wouldn't be much point in keeping these, anyway. It'd be quicker and cheaper to just go out and buy a tin of anchovies.

It's the peace and quiet I like. A place where I'm not prey to the pressures of work or the stress of being at home. It shouldn't be that way, I know, but at the moment it is, and a man's got to have his hiding place.

I think I'm calmer for it. There have been times over the past few months when I really wanted to just shout at Megan. I don't know if it's some form of post-natal depression or if she's just being too self-centred. All I know is she's not dealing with things very well. I try to do my bit, but it's not always that easy. If Megan's at home with Evie, I try to be there. Especially if she's not coping.

Her parents have been great. They know we both need our space. They've been taking Evie a couple of days a week so we can have our own time and to relax a little. It'll be for the best in the long run. Then, once Evie's sleeping better and eating solids we'll be able to get back to how we were. It just takes a little adjustment time.

I get the impression Megan resents me for coming here. I always have to bite my tongue and not mention the fact that it's usually me who gets up in the middle of the night when Evie's crying. And I'm the one who's up early. I'm the one who gives her her baths. But Megan doesn't see it that way. She just sees me popping out for a few hours and acts as if that's all I do. C'est la vie.

Things will work themselves out. They always do. Megan and I have been together long enough to know that. We've been together since school, so if we don't know each other now we never will. We'll muddle through. I said as much to Megan a couple of days ago.

She gave me that face she always gives me. The face that says expressing an opinion would make a nice change. The face that says she'd like me to be more determined and forceful. But that's just not me.

None of us can be something we're not. We'd just come across as false. And yeah, my way of dealing with things is to distance myself from them and wait until things blow over. But that's because it usually works. I don't do arguments. Never have, never will. I think I get that from my parents. They're both incredibly placid. Dad *was*. Mum and George, my step-dad get on like a house on fire. I personally can't stand the man, but even to this day I've never heard them have an argument or even a disagreement. I don't think I've actually heard my mum express an opinion on anything. She just *is*, and that's what I love about her. I can rely on her to be there, and not to judge.

Megan's parents aren't quite the same. Her mum, in particular, is much more open with her opinions. She'll happily tell people she'd do things differently, even if they haven't asked for her input or advice. And that's not to mention her magical knack for always saying the wrong thing at the wrong time and managing to become the most insensitive person in the world.

Her dad tends to take more of a backseat. I imagine it's a case of having to. I guess we're both quite similar in many ways, which is why we've tended to get on. I get on with her mum too, but it's usually a case of putting up with her as opposed to actively liking her.

I look at my watch. Half four. Mum will have dropped Evie back at the house by now. Megan's going to need a hand and I'm keen to do my bit; I just need my own space and time while I can get it. I can feel myself getting more and more short-tempered all the time, and that's not going to be good for anyone, least of all Megan and Evie.

I tend to pack light when I come out fishing. If you go further downstream, there are guys with whole trucks full of stuff. Some of them look like they're drilling for oil. I'm a purist, though. A cheap rod, some bait and a fold-up chair does me nicely. Besides which, it's a lot to carry when you're walking. One of the added benefits is it doesn't take me long to set up or pack away, either. More time to myself. More time to escape.

Escapism goes a long way, and it comes in many shapes and forms. That's not something that's easily explained to many people, though. Sometimes things aren't black and white. Whilst one person might find something wrong or immoral, to someone else it's just escapism. Horses for courses. One man's rubbish is another man's gold.

I have my own form of escapism, besides fishing. But that's not something I can tell Megan. Right now I don't think I can tell Megan anything. We've always been pretty close, but sometimes there are things a husband needs to keep from his wife. Beyond that, sometimes there are things a person needs to keep entirely to himself. After all, we all have our own secrets, don't we?

FOUR

MEGAN

Evie's finally gone down for a nap. Although it's such a battle to get her down, she tends to stay down for at least a couple of hours once she's gone. That means I get some time to myself, a chance to relax. Of course, that never actually happens. There's always hoovering to do or paperwork mounting up. Now, I've got to prepare dinner.

Just as I've opened the fridge door and have started to piece together in my mind what I could make which might come close to resembling a meal, the phone rings. I answer it without looking at the screen. It's Mum.

'I just wondered how you were both doing,' she says, despite the fact she saw us yesterday.

'We're fine. She's just gone down for her afternoon nap,' I say, as if Evie's on a schedule, which she keeps to perfectly.

'That's good. I told you she'd get the hang of it eventually.'

It's comments like that which make me wonder about my mum sometimes. Not that *I'd* get the hang of it, that I'm the one who has to go through all the work of getting Evie down to sleep. No, it's Evie's achievement for actually shutting her eyes and drifting off like every normal baby does.

'So how are you and Dad?' I ask, knowing nothing will have changed since yesterday. Nothing ever changes in their house.

'We're fine. Lauren called earlier. They're moving house, apparently.'

'Oh. That's nice,' I say, hoping she'll move on to another topic. I don't really want to hear about how well my sister's doing. I don't want to hear about her full-stop.

'Five bedrooms, three bathrooms and half an acre of land,' she says, despite the fact I haven't asked.

'Great,' I say.

'Needs a bit of work doing to it, but they've got big plans. Apparently they want to knock the downstairs bathroom through into the study and turn it into a wet room. Why you'd want one of those downstairs is anybody's guess, but it's their money. You know what Lauren's like.'

I don't know why she says things like that. I do know what Lauren's like. I know exactly what she's like, and accidentally spending a few grand on a bathroom conversion isn't the worst of it. But the way Mum says it is almost as if it's designed to get me onside, as if to pacify me, knowing my sister and I don't speak.

I don't say anything in return, but she still carries on, not getting the hint.

'Oh you should see it, Megan. It really is beautiful. It's got a thatched roof and everything.'

'Good. I'm pleased,' I say, hoping this will at least shut her up for a while. If she'd been prodding to see how I'd react, this should defuse the situation.

'And how are things with you?' she asks, as if I'm not going to notice that she's making a direct comparison between me and my sister. *Look how well she's doing, juggling a busy career and buying a five-bedroom thatched mansion while you're sitting at home unable to even cope with a baby.*

'We're all good,' I say, despite the fact she knows exactly how things are.

Mum and I have a funny relationship. I readily admit I couldn't get through most weeks without her. She's there when I need her and she does her fair share of looking after Evie for me. But at the same time there's this dirty undercurrent of knowing that I'll always play second fiddle to Lauren, who's always going to be the favoured daughter. Especially while she's 'doing so well'.

Sometimes I have half a feeling that Mum's willing me to do better, secretly hoping I'll outdo Lauren and be both the more human and more successful daughter. If truth be told, I really don't care. We're happy. Happy enough. We don't need enormous mortgages and exotic holidays to feel like we're doing well.

At least, that's the spin I put on it. Happiness is a veil

we all wear. But, deep down, we all have our problems, all have our issues, our insecurities. And they're the things that keep us going. The chinks in our armour which make us want to keep improving, that give us something to focus on as we plod on towards our inevitable deaths.

Morbid.

I don't know how, but Mum has this wonderful knack of ringing me for a nice friendly chat and inadvertently making me feel like utter shit. Maybe she's just trying to make me feel better. Perhaps she thinks hearing how well other people are doing will spur me on and make me want to do the same thing. It's funny how family politics work. How no-one ever says what they're actually thinking. How it's all smoke and mirrors and veiled comments designed to try and elicit information or gauge a reaction. It's sad really. I often wonder why people can't just come out with it and be honest with each other. It saves all the James Bond bullshit.

'Anyway, sorry to cut it short but I'm just in the middle of preparing dinner,' I say.

'Oh, no worries. Give my love to Chris and Evie, won't you? Is he fishing?'

'Yes,' I reply, trying to make it sound like it doesn't bother me in the slightest. And there I am, playing the game. Falling right into the trap and doing exactly what I hate other people doing. 'He should be back soon, though.'

'Okay. You call me if you need me, alright?'

'I know, Mum. Thanks.'

And it's times like this that I get really, really confused about my family. Is it some sort of passive-aggressive thing which makes them need to sound as though they care, when actually they're just probing and poking their noses into my business, trying to find some sort of salacious scandal or gossip?

This is one of the reasons why I've tried to keep them at arm's length, emotionally speaking. Mum's great with Evie, if a little contrary. It sounds bad saying it, but her willingness to babysit and take Evie off my hands on a regular basis has been a godsend. I won't say it's been her only redeeming feature, but it certainly helps.

I smell burning and turn around.

'Shit!' I hiss, opening the oven and flinging open the kitchen windows as I try to fan the smoke out of the room.

I sit down at the kitchen table, put my head in my hands and wish I'd never answered the phone.

FIVE

CHRIS

We've all got secrets. We've all got things we'd rather our family and friends didn't know. Not because we want to be duplicitous, but because we want to protect them. Protect them from harm. Protect them from the truth.

After all, everybody does it, don't they?

The hot water beats down on my back as I scrub under my fingernails, hard. I work the shower gel into a lather and rub it over my whole body seven or eight times, just to be sure. I wash my hair so many times I think it's going to fall out. Eventually, though, I know I'm as clean as I'm ever going to be.

I always shower in the evenings, whenever I get home from work. Or from fishing. She doesn't need to know why I'm doing it so thoroughly this time.

Megan has her secrets, too. She doesn't know that I know, but you don't live with someone for that long and not work it out. I catch the odd glimpse of something in her eyes that makes me wonder. I don't think she's been up to anything bad. That's not like Megan. Not the Megan I know. This is something deeper, something internal.

I had my suspicions shortly after Evie was born. All new parents are told to look out for the warning signs. It was almost textbook. The comments about being a bad mother, loss of memory, not taking care of herself as much as she used to. Megan always used to be a proud woman, but that seems to have gone out of the window. Sometimes she needs me to remind her to shower. We don't see friends as often as we used to. And I've noticed that she doesn't seem to be bonding as well with Evie as she should be.

I've tried bringing the subject up tactfully, but she seems to just close down and refuse to admit anything is wrong. There are times when things seem to be a bit better. Chinks of light, if you will. And it's in those moments that I hope it's all improving, that she's starting to realise she's not a bad mother or a bad person and that we can start to look forward.

I don't know if she thinks I haven't noticed, or if she's just ignoring it and hoping it'll go away. Either way, it's not helping any of us. They say you need to talk about these things, need to get them out in the open. After all, what's the point of suffering in silence? I've done all I can, but this can't be one-sided. She needs to open up and tell me what she's thinking, how she's feeling. Keeping it all wrapped up isn't going to do anyone any good, least of all her.

That said, I think I've kept my own secrets pretty well. I know that for a fact. Megan's not the sort of woman who'd react well if she suspected the truth. Not this sort of truth. She's always said she'd be able to forgive most things if I was open and honest with her about them, but I'm pretty sure this doesn't fall into the category of 'most things'. This isn't the sort of thing I can be open and honest about. This is the sort of thing that ruins lives.

Telling her certainly wouldn't be a good idea. Telling *anyone* would be a very bad idea indeed. People always say it's best to be honest, but that's absolute shit. What you don't know can't hurt you. The only risk is being found out further down the line, and making things worse by not being open from the start. But all that means is that I have to make sure no-one finds anything out further down the line. If they never find out, they never know I've been hiding anything and no-one needs to get hurt. No-one else, anyway. I need to make sure this stays as my little secret. Forever.

SIX

MEGAN

Chris gets home at about five, and I try to put on a positive face. It's the same positive face I've been putting on every day since Evie was born.

Although I feel so lonely when Chris is out, at least it means I can drop the fake smiles and stop trying to pretend everything's fine. It's amazing how much that wears you down after a while.

I'm still reeling from Mum's phone call earlier. She calls most days, especially if she's not at the house or looking after Evie. She always means well, but she's got a habit of not knowing when to stop and ending up putting her foot in it. And today she 'just happened' to mention Lauren. Again.

My sister and I haven't spoken in about four years. Not since that day at the Waterside. She and James had invited the family out for Sunday lunch. It was something we did every couple of months or so, so it didn't seem too out of the ordinary. Just after we'd ordered the meals, though, Lauren revealed the real reason for inviting everyone there. She was pregnant.

I forced the biggest smile I could imagine, and told her how happy we were for her. Chris squeezed my knee, knowing I was dying inside. We'd been trying for years to have children, but it wasn't happening. We hadn't told anyone. It just was what it was.

During the main course, Lauren asked if Chris and I were planning to have children. Lauren's always been about as tactful as a breeze block to the face, but this time she'd really excelled herself with her timing. All that was going through my mind was how she wouldn't shut the fuck up about what colour they were going to paint the nursery, what names they'd picked out, the 3D scan they'd booked. It was relentless. And it was tearing me up inside. So I told her. I told her that yes, we'd love to have children, but that we weren't able to.

For a brief moment, I thought it had finally sunk in. I thought she might have realised how selfish and thoughtless she'd been with the comments she'd made, but her brain seemed to stop short of that realisation. Instead, her response was 'Well can't you have IVF or adopt or something?'

I don't know how most people would have reacted to that. All I know is how I reacted. I stood up, remaining as calm as I could, picked my handbag up off the floor and walked out. Chris followed me, and although he didn't make any comment about what

Lauren had said, he didn't make out that I'd been unreasonable.

After the dust had settled, I probably could've forgiven it. I could have put it down to Lauren's usual insensitivity. The spoilt younger sister syndrome. But she didn't even call to apologise. That told me more about her than a lifetime of having her as my sister. That was the last day we spoke.

So no, I didn't want to hear about their new house with five bedrooms, three bathrooms and half an acre of land. I really couldn't fucking care less. I don't know what she expected me to say. 'Great, we'll have to pop in and say hi'?

My positive face clearly works, though, as Chris doesn't seem to pick up on anything. It's not something I'd want to talk about, either. Even though we have Evie now, that doesn't change what happened with Lauren beforehand.

He always seems so much more relaxed when he's been fishing. I guess it's a man thing. A chance to sit on his own, clear his head and chill out for a bit. I should be so lucky.

When dinner's over, we sit in the lounge and watch the news, as we tend to do every evening. We used to joke about the local news bulletins that come on after the national headlines, always amused at how the most boring and inane stories managed to make it onto the TV each night. It was either a local man who'd invented a new kind of nutcracker, a company manufacturing cable ties who'd just won an award or a Burnside couple who'd been without gas and hot water for the past three weeks. It tended to be the sort of stuff you wouldn't even mention to your friends in passing, never mind broadcast on the regional news.

But tonight is different.

The trailer at the start of the news programme stops us both in our tracks. We recognise where the reporter is standing before we realise what she's saying. She's walking towards the camera, down a bridleway next to the stream that runs through the village, her hands in front of her stomach, fingers intertwined, occasionally releasing them to gesture loosely as she speaks.

Her words seem to blur into one huge fuzzy noise, as she speaks for barely five seconds about the body of the young boy that's been found in this 'sleepy, peaceful village'.

'What the hell?' I say, eventually. 'Here? Did you hear about this?'

Chris sits staring at the screen, his eyes glassy. 'No. Nothing. I've not even looked at my phone. It was on silent.'

I can tell what's going through his mind without even asking. The chances of the boy being one of his students or ex-students is high. Chris has taught practically everyone under the age of eighteen within a three or four mile radius at one point or another. This is a small place, a tight community.

Chris picks up his mobile, taps the screen a few times and puts it to his ear.

I give him a quizzical look.

'Calling Rebecca,' he says. His boss. The headteacher at the school. 'Rebecca. Hi. I just saw the news. What's happened?'

Rebecca's voice is loud on the other end of the phone, and I can just about make out her saying he had only been found an hour or two earlier, and that they'd tried to keep it quiet until friends and relatives had been told, but that the press had somehow got wind of it.

'Who is it?' he asks, his voice shaking as he leaves the lounge and walks into the hallway.

I don't hear Rebecca's answer, but I see Chris stop in his tracks, his shoulders and upper back sagging. And in that moment I know something isn't right.

SEVEN

MEGAN

It took Chris almost twenty minutes to speak to me. When he finally did, he told me all about the sort of boy Riley Markham had been. Not the most gifted student academically speaking, but far from struggling. He'd been the archetypal cheeky chappy; he'd had a good telling off once or twice and seemed keener on playing football at lunchtime than paying attention in some classes. But he was the sort of student teachers tended to have a bit of a soft spot for. It seemed Chris was no different.

Rebecca seemed to know more than the news reporter, thank God. It seemed it had only made the local bulletin right at the last possible minute, and had managed to come in too late for the national news. That would all change for the News at Ten, we were told. And they were right. The late national evening news bulletins had it as their second item. It wasn't often that seven-year-olds were found dead.

Chris said those words to me, paraphrasing Rebecca, but he didn't say the last one. I filled it in for him. He corrected me.

Not dead. Murdered.

Rebecca didn't have the precise details but, from what she'd managed to find out, Riley's killer had attempted to strangle him, and had also hit him over the head with some sort of blunt object. She mentioned blood at the scene.

I don't know what to think when I'm hearing these words. As a mother, it should fill me with horror and revulsion, with thoughts of how I might feel if that was my child. But I'm not sure I feel any differently to how I would have done before Evie was born.

It's a tragedy. An absolute tragedy. No-one deserves to go through what Riley Markham's family are going through right now. But I hate my present situation for not making me feel far more empathetic.

Chris has dropped hints once or twice that I might want to see a doctor. I left him in no doubt that wouldn't be happening. I'm not having Evie taken away from me or anyone thinking I'm a bad mother. Lots of mums struggle after the birth of their children. And most of them come through the other side. Most of them.

It's a shock to the system, having a child. In every conceivable way. Everything in your life changes. People told us before Evie was born that would be the case, and we believed them, but we could never have known to what extent that would be true. It changes everything.

Chris has been distant ever since. We used to be close — we'd always been close — but that stopped almost immediately after Evie was born. It was as if we were only connected by this little screaming bag of flesh, rather than any direct connection between the two of us.

When we found out about Riley's death last night, I felt so sorry for Chris. I know what a dedicated teacher he is, and how much he cares for every child that passes through his class. He spoke fondly of Riley, and I got the impression that the boy was one he'd helped on a number of occasions.

He asked me if I thought he should go round and speak to the parents, offer his condolences. I told him it would probably be best to wait, to allow them some time and space. I can't even begin to imagine what they're going through, but I don't think for one minute I'd want every man and his dog turning up on my doorstep. They'll have enough to worry about at the moment.

The texts and phone calls started coming in thick and fast. This is a tight community, and bad news travels quickly. Everyone always seems to know everyone else's news before they do, and I've got a few suspicions as to who might have tipped off the press almost instantly. I don't say any of this to Chris, though. I need to try and stay strong and calm for him.

He had a haunted look in his eyes all night. It reminded me of those old war veterans you see in films, their eyes hazing over with painful memories as they recount tales of battle and bloodshed. He seemed genuinely troubled by his thoughts.

He talked in his sleep again last night. I didn't think much of it at the time — it's something he does fairly regularly — but this time he sounded pained, anguished. I couldn't quite make out the words, but he was mumbling something about guilt and karma. It wasn't the content that worried me, but his tone of voice. He sounded like he was on the edge of a breakdown. I don't know what he was dreaming about, but he woke up this morning seemingly normal — apart from the obvious effect last night's news had had on him.

He said he wanted to go and see Riley's family. I wasn't sure that was a good idea — not so soon after the event — but he was insistent. I had the feeling it might help him somehow, perhaps provide some sort of comfort.

Riley's death has been playing on my mind this morning. It didn't seem to affect me in the way I would have expected when I heard the news last night. Today, I'm starting to wonder if it hadn't sunk in until now. I've been looking at Evie differently, my brain trying to process what a mother could possibly be feeling at a time like this. A normal mother.

I've been trying to distract myself with household chores. The kitchen's sparkling clean, every ornament in the house has been dusted and once I've put the bin out I'll start wiping down the cupboard fronts. I poke my head around the doorway to the living room and see Evie sitting in her bouncer, chewing on a toy, happily watching *This Morning* on the TV.

I gather up the black plastic sack, tie the end, and unlock the back door. An uneasy feeling hits me as I open the lid of the wheeliebin. I can't explain it, but it's similar to the sense of dread you get immediately before something horrible happens.

As I open the lid and spot the lone piece of blue and white fabric between the two black sacks at the bottom of the bin, I pause for a moment. I reach inside, grab hold of it and pull it out.

It's a baseball cap. Far too small for an adult; this is a kid's cap. It's blue and white, with the number 82 stitched onto the front. Mostly blue and white. The rest of it is stained deep red, almost black. It's blood.

EIGHT

CHRIS

I must have been sitting in the car for a good ten or fifteen minutes, just watching. I still can't bring myself to open the door, get out and walk up the path to Riley's parents' house. On the face of it, it sounds like the simplest thing to do but I can't bring myself to do it.

Every teacher feels responsible when something happens to a kid they've taught, whether it was their fault or not. It's the duty of care that's drummed into us all, no matter how much we have to rally against it at times. Because where does that duty of care stop? In a community like this, it can smother you as easily as protect you. Everyone knows everyone. Everyone relies on everyone. It's a finely balanced ecosystem which can be brought crashing down with relative ease.

And this might just do it.

This place has always felt claustrophobic. It's home, of course, but it's stifling. Not being able to walk down the street whilst remaining anonymous, not being able to be yourself. Not being allowed to have secrets.

Things need to change around here. It's no good living in each other's pockets all the time. It doesn't help anyone. Sometimes, people need to cut loose.

This is what these sorts of events do to your brain, it seems. I can't think clearly — I haven't been able to for a long time — and it's going to ruin me if I'm not careful.

It feels strange to say, but Evie brought such a huge change and upheaval into our lives that it's made me reassess things. I can see life from another angle now. It's opened my mind. It's made me think much more clearly, as well as having confused everything else at the same time.

Time on my own is crucial. I need to do it to keep my own thoughts at bay. I need the time and space to have a calm word with my inner demons. If I didn't get the time alone... Well, I don't know. I think I'd probably snap. And that wouldn't be good for anyone. It would break Megan to know how I really feel at times, to know what goes through my mind. And the ramifications of that would have a lifelong impact on Evie. How would she cope without her father?

It doesn't bear thinking about. And that's why I must act normal. That's why I have to make it look as though everything's fine, as if I'm not carrying a dark secret around with me which threatens to tear my family apart and split a fissure through the middle of this community.

I look up at the house again. There's a police officer on

the door, who seems as though he hasn't moved in the whole time I've been sitting here. He hasn't glanced in my direction once. An older couple I don't recognise walk up to the front door, exchange a few words with the police officer and press the doorbell. The door opens a few seconds later, and they walk inside. I don't see who opens the door. I'm thankful for that, in a way. Seeing the sheer pain etched on the face of Riley's parents would break me.

I need a release. I need *the* release.

I'd been tempted for a while. I'm sure the thought crosses everyone's mind at some point or another. You see someone who fits the bill and you just... Just ignore it. Because it's not the done thing, is it? But for some of us that temptation builds and builds until you can't handle it any more. And you have to do it.

The guilt you feel afterwards is immeasurable. After the immediate exhilaration, of course. The thrill of the chase finally being over. The hunter having snared his prey. But the prey often makes it far too easy. It spoils the enjoyment somewhat. Which means there's still an itch there to be scratched, still that desire for doing it all over again. Raise the stakes this time. Make it harder. Make it riskier. Because that's the only way I'm going to be able to get what I need out of this.

My heart's racing as I think about it, and I can feel the butterflies in my chest. Just the thought of it makes me want to wriggle free and get out of here. I shouldn't be thinking these thoughts. Not here. Not after how my actions — my addictions — have affected Riley's family.

How can anyone be expected to carry on after that? How would I feel if it were my own family?

At times, when I'm thinking normally and rationally, I start to wonder about myself. I clearly have a conscience. I have love for my family. So why do I still have this horrendous, grotesque itch that needs to be scratched? How can I possibly be two completely different people at the same time? And what makes the other side come out?

I can only find these answers from within myself. There is no other option. There's no-one I can speak to about it. The truth cannot possibly come out.

I turn the key in the ignition, put on my seatbelt, put the car into gear and drive off down the road.

NINE

MEGAN

I don't know how long I stand there holding the blood-stained cap, as everything seems to become a blur. I can hear the blood pulsing in my ears, feel my heart fluttering. In my heart of hearts, I know what this is. I know whose it is. I don't think I've ever seen the cap before, but at the same time I instinctively know the story behind it. And I know who put it there. How else would a blood-stained young boy's baseball cap get in our wheeliebin?

There is only one reason, but I can't quite convince myself it's true. I have to believe it isn't. I need to.

There's no way into our back garden from the road. The houses are so tightly packed together, we have to take the bin out through the garage on bin day. It's a constant source of frustration — one of those things we overlooked when we bought the house, but which has since become the bane of our lives. Chris, in his usual let's-look-at-the-positives style, declared it 'great for security'. And it's exactly that sentiment which is now beginning to worry me.

The fence around the garden is high, and the bushes are dense and prickly. I've never been a keen gardener, so we decided to leave the perimeter more or less as it was. They say you can't stop a determined burglar — the best you can hope for is to send them next door — and I don't think any burglar in their right mind would prefer our practical assault course. There is no way in, nor out. I certainly wouldn't like to try it myself.

Most of the time, that's great. But not now. This isn't right. Could someone have got in from outside the property and dumped the cap in our bin? No. No way. It's not as if it was flung in there when the bin was last out on the street ready for collection, either. It's nestled on top of a couple of bin bags that've been put in there since the last collection — while the bin was in our garden. There's no way that cap could have got in there. Unless...

I hear the faint ringing of the doorbell inside the house. I throw the cap back into the bin and wipe my hands on the front of my clothes. There's nothing on them, but all the same I feel dirty. Filthy. Diseased. I go back into the house, and can hear Evie starting to cry. I get a sudden stabbing of guilt as I realise I left her inside on her own while I was out here.

'It's alright, darling. Mummy won't be a second,' I call through to the living room as I go to the front door. I turn the key, pull down the handle and open the door to find two police officers standing there. One man, one woman. The woman speaks.

'Hello, are you Mrs Megan Miller?'

'Yes,' I say, my voice faint and weak.

'I'm PC Smith, this is PC Laurent. Can we speak to your husband, please?'

TEN

MEGAN

'He's not here,' are the words I just about manage to squeeze out through my tight lips.

'Do you know where he's gone or when he'll be back?'

'He'll probably only be an hour or so at most,' I reply. I don't know why I didn't tell them where he is. Instinctively, I feel a need to protect him. 'What's this all about?'

'We just need to ask him for some information that might be linked to an incident that happened yesterday. You probably heard about it.'

I nod. 'The little boy. Riley.'

'Chris was his teacher, I hear.'

I nod again. 'Last year. The one that's just finished.'

She smiles. 'We're looking to speak to anyone who might have known Riley and could help us find out what happened to him. We'll pop back a bit later, but if he comes home before then could you ask him to give me a call, please?'

She hands me a business card, with her name, rank and mobile number underneath the county's police insignia.

'I will. Thank you.'

'No problem. We'll let you get on with your day. Sounds like you've got enough on your plate.'

She signals with her eyes towards the inside of the house. It's only then that I recognise the sound of Evie screaming in the living room behind me.

'Yes. Sorry. She's teething. Lack of sleep. You know how it is.'

She half-smiles, half-laughs. 'I don't, fortunately. And I don't think I want to, either. I'll stick with cats.'

'Don't blame you,' I say. 'I'll get Chris to call you when he's home.'

When they're gone, I stand in the hallway and try to compose myself. This is too much all at once. My mind wasn't in the right place to begin with. Now we've got the bombshell of a young boy being murdered in the village, the bloodstained cap in the bin, the police turning up on our doorstep and that *bloody incessant screaming*.

I march into the living room and yell 'What?!' at the top of my voice. Evie looks at me, a confused and panicked look in her eyes. Then her lip starts trembling and she starts crying again, but a different sort of cry. Instantly, I feel like the worst person in the world. I go over and pick her up, put her to my chest and try to comfort her.

'Ssshh, there we are. Mummy's sorry. I'm sorry.'

After a few minutes, I manage to calm her down. I know I can't let this all get the better of me, can't let it affect Evie, but it's so hard. I put her back down in her bouncer, give her a toy or two to play with and go into the kitchen.

I lean on the worktop and try to catch my breath. This is too much, too fast. I'm swinging between utter confusion and knowing that secretly, deep down, I *want* to be confused. I want it to make no sense. Because the alternative is that it all makes perfect sense.

Twenty-four hours ago, things were far from perfect. But they were a hell of a lot closer to it than they are now. A young boy, murdered. A boy who'd been taught by Chris. Chris, who was fishing, alone, with no alibi, when it happened. And the bloodstained cap. In our bin. It all points one way, but I can't think of it as an option. Can I?

I have to know, though. I need to. I can't go round to Riley's parents' house and ask them if he had a blue and white baseball cap.

It could all have a perfectly innocent explanation. There are sick fucks out there who kill children. We all know that. And each child who dies will have had a number of teachers. Those teachers have families. This time, we're that family.

And the cap? What's the innocent explanation for that? We don't have young boys. Maybe Chris found it when he was out somewhere. Perhaps when he was fishing. He's the sort of person who hates litter. He can't stand things being where they shouldn't be. Maybe he picked it up and brought it home to put it in the bin. At the time, he wouldn't have even realised the significance. He probably forgot all about it. If I mentioned it to him now, he might make the link. It could be little Riley Markham's cap *and* not throw suspicion straight at Chris's door. It's entirely possible. And together we could explain that, hand the cap over to the police and they could use it to find Riley's killer.

That would be the logical, sensible thing to do. But there's a lingering, nagging doubt at the back of my mind. Something that says that really wouldn't be a good idea. Something that says I need to protect my family.

They say you can't ignore your gut. That even though pure logic and available evidence could well point in the absolute opposite direction, what you feel in the pit of your stomach is often more right than anything else. That sort of instinct has served me well in my life so far, but now it threatens to bring everything I've worked for crashing down around me. Because my instinct says I can't possibly confront Chris with the bloodstained baseball cap, and I certainly can't take it to the police. And that realisation fills me with dread.

Evie's quiet. For now. I decide to put the kettle on. I need to maintain some semblance of normality.

As the kettle boils, my phone vibrates and plays a stab of the theme tune from the *BBC News* programme. It's the noise it makes when a news alert pops up.

I look at my phone.

Young boy murdered in small village named as seven-year-old Riley Markham, police say.

So it's official. They've named him. That means his extended family and loved ones have all been told. Dozens of people have just had their lives brought crashing down around them. Their entire existence paused at that moment in time. There will only ever be Before and After.

I tap the pop-up and the news article loads. I start to read, the words all blurring into one grey mass.

Until I get further down the page and see the young, smiling face of Riley Markham looking up at me, his bright blue eyes peering out from under a distinctive and familiar baseball cap.

ELEVEN

FIVE YEARS EARLIER

The waiting room feels cold. I bring my hands across my chest and rub my upper arms. It's mid-July, but I'm freezing. Middle-aged women sit around me, fanning themselves with paper fans. Men sit spreadeagled in shorts and sunglasses, those daft toe-splitting flip-flops dangling off the end of their feet.

I turn to Chris. He looks at me and smiles, and places a reassuring hand on my thigh. He squeezes. I feel instantly warmer.

It doesn't last long, though. I know deep down what's going to be said today isn't going to be good news. We've been trying for three years. We have sex every other day — sometimes every day — but still nothing. I don't need a doctor to tell me what's wrong. Sometimes you just know in your heart. It doesn't feel right. Doesn't feel realistic, no matter how much I want it to happen.

We've read all the books, bookmarked all the websites. I've tried everything. Even the relaxation and mindfulness techniques which are meant to reduce stress — a big reason why many couples have trouble conceiving. I even did meditation sessions. At one point I must have had a dozen apps on my phone, including one which was just daily sessions of some bloke talking soothingly over Tibetan pipe music. It was bizarre, but also strangely relaxing.

The condescending little shit with the irritating voice is a big advocate of visualisation. He says if you want something to happen, you have to be able to see it, to visualise it. And try as I might, no matter how vividly I brought to mind images of me and Chris with a house full of giggling, happy children, it just didn't feel *right*. I knew I was only projecting my own desires. I wasn't looking into the future. I knew, deep down, it would never happen.

And that's why I know today isn't going to be good news. One ray of hope that the websites and books all tell you is that practically no couples are ever told they *definitely* can't have children. The doctors just say your chances are greatly reduced, or that you should assume it won't happen. The papers are full of stories of families who have been told one or more partners is infertile, only to end up popping out quadruplets a few months later.

But what can you say to someone who's given up all hope?

I know they'll mention IVF today. It's bound to happen. Especially after three years of trying. And I know what the maths are there, too. Twenty grand down the drain and our chances of conception raised to 5%. Then come the other dreaded words that no person who's desperate to have children ever wants to hear. Fostering. Adoption.

It's not simply a case of wanting to look after a child. If that were the case, I'd become a babysitter or go to work at a nursery. It's not even comparable to having a little person around the house who's your own flesh and blood. Someone who is entirely made up of DNA and genetic material that is half you, half the person you love and have chosen to spend the rest of your life with. That little person who is, quite literally, scientifically speaking, 50% you. The only person in the world who is. Even your own parents don't count. They aren't 50% you; you are 50% them.

Having your own children is seeing your own genetic existence extended by another eighty or ninety years. I think I read somewhere that a child born today has a life expectancy of over one hundred. That's how incredible medical science is. That something which wasn't even so much as a cluster of cells just over nine months ago can be more or less assured of a century of NHS-supported existence. That it can go from being a tiny, slimy pink ball to a dying adult with great-grandchildren over the space of ten decades.

But in our case, and in tens of thousands of others, we can't even get past that first stage. The easy bit. Smashing a sperm into an egg. An accidental collision. A tiny, insignificant event which is the starting point for everything else that is to come. The birth, the birthdays, the schooldays, the friendships, the jobs, the marriages, the grandchildren, the heartache and the loss. Everything results from that meeting of two cells.

They can collide particles at extraordinary velocity inside collision chambers in Switzerland, but they can't manage this.

And that's the sanctity of life in a nutshell, isn't it? That's why our children are so precious. That's why you throw yourself in front of a bus to save a toddler. That's why you walk out into the road so a woman with a pushchair doesn't have to. That's why kids go free. Because without them we have no future. We, ourselves, cannot live on.

And that's why it feels so completely and utterly devastating to have slowly come to the realisation that I can't — won't — be a part of that. Instead, I'll be some sort of cast-off from society. The person nature decided wasn't good enough to join in the propagation of the species. The person who, try as they might, would never see their legacy live on. The woman who'd die without anyone to talk about her. Who'd never come up in conversation years later. No fond memories, no tall tales. Just wiped from existence as if I'd never been there in the first place.

Chris taps my knee. 'Come on. That's us,' he says, as he gets up and walks towards the consulting rooms. I force a smile and swallow hard. Then I pick up my bag and push myself to my feet, my knees trembling and my heart fluttering in my chest.

I feel like the condemned man walking to the gallows.

TWELVE

MEGAN

Evie's screams rattle around my skull as I try to calm her down. She didn't want to be cuddled, didn't want to be held, so I sat her on my lap. She didn't like that either, so I laid her down on the floor. When that failed too, I sat her in front of her toys. She stopped crying for just long enough to reach across for one and land face-first in the carpet. Cue screaming.

I can feel my anger and frustration rising as I rub her back and make soothing noises to her, even though all I want to do is scream *SHUT THE FUCK UP!*

Sometimes, nothing seems to work. I go round and round in circles trying all the usual methods: singing, cooing, bouncing, distracting, showing her her favourite toys. But absolutely nothing stops her crying. Eventually she seems to give up and lay there gurgling, as if exhausted by all the exertion of screaming.

I don't know why she does it. In many ways I don't

care. I just want it to stop. I've tried good old Dr Google. What new mum hasn't? There are pages and pages of shit on the internet about different methods of getting a baby to sleep, why babies cry, what's normal and abnormal. The truth of the matter is, there's no such thing as normal. Any parent will tell you that. But it doesn't mean I'm happy to let her sit there screaming.

Dad suggested taking her to a doctor, which wasn't something I was keen on. I'm not about to go up to a medical professional and admit I'm a failure as a mother. Fortunately, Mum didn't like the idea either, and said something about all babies being different. That you have to follow your own instinct and do whatever feels right at the time.

The only problem is my instincts are all over the place, not to mention the rest of my mind.

The one good thing about Evie's screaming is that it's distracting me from what's really going on inside my head. When I close my eyes, all I can see is Riley Markham's face smiling from underneath that baseball cap. The blue and white one with the number 82 stitched onto it. The one that's nestled inside my wheelie bin, stained with blood. With what I can only assume is Riley's blood.

It's not often you pray that someone's broken into your property, but I really hope that's the case. I pray to whatever higher being there is that someone — Riley's killer — was so desperate to make his escape that he jumped a few fences and ran through people's gardens to get away, and that on the way he dumped Riley's cap in our wheelie bin.

That should be the logical explanation. That should be the conclusion that I come to automatically, with nothing else even worth considering. But deep down I know it's not true. I know from the expression on Chris's face when I look at him, from the way he fidgets agitatedly in his sleep, from the ways in which he's changed in recent times. I know something's not right.

You don't spend your entire life with someone without knowing deep down when something is wrong. History's full of women who claim they had no idea their husband was the person he actually was. They're in denial. Their brain was hiding all the signs from them, trying to protect them. It's a coping mechanism. If you couldn't handle the truth were it to come out, your brain won't let you discover the truth. Everything that points towards it will somehow be stretched or distorted or spun into something else. Something which has far more innocent, far less dangerous implications.

I wonder how long my brain's been doing that to me, and why it's stopped now. Is this really the first time I've suspected something odd about Chris? The first time I've known he's hiding a dark secret? I can't say for sure, but if I dig down deep enough I suspect not.

My heart almost bursts out of my chest as I think about Evie. Is he a danger to our daughter? How could I live with myself if I didn't tell someone what I'd found and Evie ended up coming to some harm? If not Evie, another child. More children.

It could have been an accident. He might've been talking to Riley, or accidentally knocked him over. People do that, don't they? You see it all the time on TV and in films. Someone accidentally dies and it looks as though the other person did it, so they have to hide it as if they *were* guilty. But they're not.

Or it's all some huge elaborate setup. Or it's the killer who decided to choose our bin to dump the cap in, coincidence of coincidences. And why not? Most people in this village know each other. Even if he picked a bin at random, the killer would be hard pushed to find an owner who didn't have at least some tenuous link to Riley Markham, I'm sure.

It's all going round and round in my head, over and over again, and I know it's logical to take the cap to the police. If it's Chris, he'll be dealt with. Our lives will be torn apart but justice will be done. Won't it? What will happen to Evie? What if it wasn't him? He'll be arrested, certainly. And even if he's innocent that's sure to wreck his career as a teacher. Everyone in the village will know what happened and his name will never be completely cleared. There'll always be the people who think something happened, who think he got away with it. And even those who know the truth will still associate his name with what happened. Things will never be the same again. Evie will never hear the last of it. She doesn't need that sort of start in life.

And even if things could — somehow — be kept confidential, can we rely on the police to get to the truth? To do things properly? I'd love to think so, but I have one huge nagging doubt.

I don't trust the police. I can't. Not since what happened.

It's been a long time since then, I tell myself. It was a different part of the world. A different culture. Different ways of doing things. Those sorts of things are far less likely to happen over here. Police corruption might have been big business here years ago, but it's got to be better now. We're always told it's better. But that still doesn't help my inherent distrust of anyone in a uniform.

We're all affected by our past experiences, but I need to think clearly and logically about this. We have the best judicial system in the world over here. Miscarriages of justice are rare. Aren't they?

THIRTEEN

EIGHT YEARS EARLIER

The sun beats down on the back of our necks as we try to hug the shade. Anything after ten o'clock in the morning is unbearable in Oualidia at this time of year. The Moroccan coast has played host to a heatwave for the past three or four weeks, according to the locals. People joke that no-one comes home from their honeymoon with a tan as they're too busy staying in their hotel room, and we may well have that problem for very different reasons. Air conditioning.

When we have dared to venture out we've been hopping from bar to bar, necking cool drinks and enjoying the fans blowing slightly less warm air across us.

Believe it or not, the temperature has dropped a little today — it's only in the high thirties as opposed to the mid forties — so we decided we'd head to the market.

It's a kaleidoscope of colour, with just about everything you could name for sale somewhere. From carpets and spices to building materials and electronic gadgets, it's like a noisy, muddled up, slightly dirty outdoor department store. I've never seen anything like it in my life.

This isn't a browser's market. You need to know where you're going and what you're buying, because if you slow down at any point to look at what's on offer you get jostled from side to side by people pushing past you to get to where they're going. It's brash, it's loud and it's in your face. But I love it.

The heat within the market is stifling. It's hot and humid, the combination of the late morning heat and the hundreds — if not thousands — of people who are crammed in here to pick up the week's bargains.

After half an hour or so, it all gets too much and we decide to leave. We nip through a gap between two stalls and leave the cover of the market, panting as the outside temperature feels so much lower than it did in there. It must be pushing forty celsius out here, but it feels like a cool English autumn to us.

We look both ways and cross the road, and it's only when we reach the other side that we hear the shouting. I turn to look at what's going on, and it's then that I feel the large hand on my shoulder.

The voice shouts at me in Arabic. I don't understand a word, but I know it doesn't sound good.

It takes me a moment to realise that the men who've stopped us are police officers. I'm confused. Is jaywalking illegal in Morocco?

They push us further away from the road and stand us up against a grey wall.

'English?' one of the officers, who I can now see has a rather impressive bushy moustache, asks Chris. Neither of them speak to me.

'Yes,' he replies. I can tell he's shaken.

'Open your lady's bag,' the same officer says to him.

Chris processes this for a moment, then does as he's told. I hand him the drawstring bag I've had slung over my right shoulder since we headed out this morning. As soon as I bring the bag in front of me to hand it to Chris, I can see that the mouth of the bag is more open than I left it. I make sure I always pull the strings tight. Chris knows this, and a look flashes between us as he hands the bag over to the moustachioed officer.

The officer looks me up and down, sniffs through one nostril then pulls apart the jaws of the bag, plunging his arm inside and pulling out what looks like quite an expensive watch. If that's come from the market it'll be anything but expensive, but the forgeries are getting better and better these days.

'What is this?' he asks me, dangling the watch in front of my face. I can almost smell it.

'I don't know. I didn't put it there,' I say.

I catch Chris's eye, and he knows in an instant that I'm telling the truth. We both have a very uneasy feeling about this.

'You lie,' the officer says. 'Turn around.'

The next thing I know, we're up against the wall, our

hands are in handcuffs and we're being led towards a police van.

We spent the next two hours sitting in stuffy, stinking, dusty cells without any food or water. There were many points where I thought I was going to pass out. Eventually, someone opens my cell door and indicates for me to stand and follow him.

He leads me through to what I can only assume is an interview room. Chris is already seated in there when I arrive.

We sit in silence for a few moments, before the moustachioed officer enters the room and sits opposite us.

'You are aware that theft is a very serious crime in Morocco?'

I say nothing, but Chris nods. I'm fairly sure we should have access to a solicitor. We would in England. Surely it's the same here?

'How did you find our cells?' the officer asks me.

I don't know how to answer this. 'Not very nice,' I say, eventually.

'You do not want to spend next ten years in one, no?'

'No. No I don't.'

He sniffs through one nostril again, then leans forward, his hands clasped together on the table.

'But this is what I must do when people commit theft. This is my job.'

'I didn't st—'

Chris places a hand on my knee to stop me talking. I immediately get the impression he was in here for some time before me. These two have already spoken before.

'Fortunately, there are certain... arrangements... that we can come to. You are very sorry for what you did, yes?'

Chris taps me on the knee.

I blink a few times. 'Yes. Yes, I'm very sorry.'

The officer nods and strokes his moustache. 'Good. Good. And you would like to be released now, yes? You would like to continue your holiday?'

I nod. 'Yes. I would.'

'Sometimes these incidents can be bad for diplomatic relations,' he says. I get the feeling he's said this many times before. 'If you have money, I can release you.'

I look at him. He's asking for a bribe.

'Processing fee,' he says, smiling, as he catches the look that crosses my face.

I swallow. 'How much?'

'Five thousand Dirham.'

I almost choke. That's around four hundred pounds.

'We don't have that much on us,' I say. Our hotel is all-inclusive, so we only brought enough cash for the odd visit to the market or visits to some of the bars in town.

'How much?' he asks.

I look at Chris. Chris doesn't look back at me. Instead, he answers. 'Just under two thousand.'

The officer seems to consider this for a moment. Then, silently, he curls his lower lip and nods, his eyes closed.

He puts his hand out and rubs his thumb against his fingertips.

Chris takes the cash out of his pocket and places it on the table. The officer picks it up and counts it out.

'One thousand, nine hundred forty Dirham.'

'Yes. It's all we have,' Chris says.

'But price is five thousand Dirham.'

'It's all we have.'

'We still need three thousand sixty Dirham.'

'We don't have it. This is everything we have.'

'Perhaps for three thousand, your wife...' He makes a hand and mouth signal to symbolise oral sex, then gives us his biggest, dirtiest grin.

Chris and I sit silent and shocked for a moment.

'It is a joke,' the officer says, after what seems like an age. 'One thousand, nine hundred forty. Okay. Come.'

He pockets the cash, stands and opens the door. Chris looks at me, then we stand and follow him.

When we get out into the main body of the police station, the officer calls to one of his colleagues and they speak in loud Arabic.

'We wait here. He will open the doors.'

Chris stands closest to the door, and I behind him. As we stand and wait, I start to feel my dress being lifted. The light fabric brushes against my backside and I'm frozen to the spot. I can't move. Can't speak. Then I feel the officer's hand on my backside, two fingers parting the cheeks as he manoeuvres my underwear and slips a third inside me. I feel his breath, hot and sticky on the back of my neck.

Chris is standing right here, in front of me. If he turned around, would he see it? Why won't he turn around? What good would it do?

It lasts only a few seconds, but it feels like an age. Then, just as suddenly as it started, he removes his hand and my dress falls back around my legs.

The other officer opens the doors and lets us out into the sticky afternoon air. As we step outside, I turn around to look at the moustachioed officer, who stands in the doorway with his hands on his hips.

'Give my regards to England,' he says, before putting his middle finger in his mouth.

FOURTEEN

MEGAN

The sound of the front door closing jolts me awake, before a huge surge of adrenaline runs through me. All the thoughts hit me at a million miles an hour. Where's Evie? How did I fall asleep? Shit, Chris is home.

I look down and see Evie asleep in her Moses basket. I don't remember putting her there, but I've been so tired recently. Chris walks into the living room. I try to look normal, try not to look as if I'm staring into the eyes of a potential child killer.

'Hi,' he says, before sitting down in an armchair. 'She been down long?'

'A little while,' I say, although I really have no clue. 'How did it go?'

He shrugs. 'About as well as can be expected.'

'They must be devastated.'

'Yeah. They are.'

I watch his face carefully 'The police called round while you were out.'

He looks at me. 'Oh?'

'They wanted to speak to you about Riley.' I pause for a couple of moments. 'They said they want to speak to anyone who knew him. To try and piece together what might have happened.'

'Oh. Oh right.'

There's no way I can deny the flash of relief that crossed his face when he found out the police wanted to talk to lots of people. But then again, who wouldn't be a bit panicked if they came home and found out the police had been looking for them? Surely the only person who wouldn't be surprised is the killer.

'Tea?' he asks.

'Please.'

He gets up and walks into the kitchen. After a few seconds, he calls me. I go through into the kitchen and see him tidying away my breakfast plates.

'How many times do we have to go through all this?' he says. 'It's not difficult to tidy up after yourself.'

'It is when you have to look after a baby, actually.'

'Come off it, Megs. She's asleep. It only takes a minute to tidy up. If you're not asleep as well, that is.'

I put my hands on my hips. 'And what's that meant to mean?'

'Exactly what I said. Maybe if you weren't sleeping on the sofa and actually tried to get the house in order, this place wouldn't look like a bomb's hit it.'

I don't know what's got into Chris, but he's rarely this unreasonable.

'Chris, I sat down for five minutes. For the first five minutes today — probably this week.'

'Come off it. Evie doesn't do anything. She just shits and cries and sleeps. You're bored, that's what it is.'

'I beg your pardon?'

'You need something to focus your mind on. We all do. Maybe it's about time you went back to work. All this leisure time isn't good for you.'

I really can't believe where this is coming from. The man who gets six weeks off work and spends five and a half of them out fishing, before cramming all his planning into the last few days. And he's got the cheek to lecture me about going back to work?

'Leisure time? Chris, I get no leisure time whatsoever. I spend my entire day looking after Evie and trying — *trying* — to keep the house looking slightly more appealing than Beirut. And what have you done for us recently?'

'This again,' he says, ignoring my question and deciding instead to empty the dishwasher.

'I mean it, Chris.'

He rounds on me. 'I've got enough to deal with at the moment, in case you hadn't noticed. Or have you been too wrapped up in yourself to have bothered to think about anyone else?'

I try to hold my temper. 'Oh no. Oh no you don't. You don't get to use that. You've been like this for months now, if not more. You can't use Riley as some sort of "I get to do what I want" bargaining tool. That's not how it works.'

Chris stops and looks at me. 'A bargaining tool? Do you think that's what it is? Seriously, Megan, you need to take a look inside your head at some point. You know, I'm actually pretty worried about the sorts of things Evie is picking up from you. Maybe I should stay home more in the holidays. Maybe I should do the parenting and you can go out. Get a job. See some friends. Breathe in some fresh air. Sitting around the house all day seems to have addled your brain.'

'I do not "sit around the house all day". I cook. I clean. I look after Evie. Or at the very least I *try* to do all those things. And what help do I get from you?'

'Well pardon me for having a bit of time off in between working twelve-hour days the rest of the year. I can sit around here and fester with you if you prefer? Or maybe pile a load more work on top of myself and end up snapping and losing the plot? Which would you prefer? Sooner or later you've got to face it, Megan. You have it pretty easy.'

I have a thousand things I could say back to that, but I choose not to. I don't see what good it'll do me. He's too stuck in his ways to accept anything but what he's already accepted as fact.

I shake my head, turn around and go back into the living room to look after our daughter.

FIFTEEN

CHRIS

It isn't doing Megan any good sitting around the house, moping.

I almost snapped. I almost went for her. I was *this* close to breaking and doing something I would have regretted. And I wonder how long I can carry on before I finally do it. Before I can't keep that side of me at bay any longer.

There are ways I can keep it down, though. Now I have a channel for my frustrations. It's wrong — it's so wrong — but it's got to be better than the alternative. If the truth got out it would ruin my family, but in many ways I'm protecting them. It gives me a huge release and ensures I don't take out my frustrations on them.

It's like a dog that needs exercising. A big, black dog. If you don't let it out to run around and kill rabbits every once in a while, it'll go for you or your family instead. So fuck the rabbits. They're cannon fodder.

Heartless? In some ways. But I prefer to look at the deeper repercussions. This road is far less bumpy than it looks. It's certainly smoother than the alternative. And when you're only faced with two options, what are you expected to do? Snap your fingers and hope it all goes away?

Sometimes I think of what I stand to lose. And then I realise that I would lose it all anyway if I didn't keep the demons at bay. At least I've found a way to hide my secret. For now. I don't think anyone suspects. And yes, people will get hurt. People will get hurt either way. But this way, I hope, I can keep it to a minimum and keep the hurt well away from my own family. At the end of the day, you've got to look after number one.

The kitchen starts to feel colder, and I decide to make myself that cup of tea. Look at me. Mister Normal Family Man. What a joke.

I'm sure everyone else sees us as the perfect close-knit household. The stay-at-home mum and the village teacher who spends the holidays with his young family. In many ways there's nothing I'd like more than to go into the living room right now, pick Evie up and give her a huge, warm hug. But, as bad as it sounds, I don't want to face Megan at the moment. Sometimes we need our time apart to cool down.

It doesn't make me a bad father. At least I don't think it does. I look after my family in other ways. I provide for them. I protect them. I protect them from the truth. And that's worth more than any hug in front of bloody television cartoons.

I know I need to keep a lid on my anger and frustrations. I can't let it boil over and become visible. I've become accustomed to that as a teacher, so it's something I've had a lot of practise doing. There've been so many times I've just wanted to smash their heads off a wall when they've done something stupid, but you can't. You have to push it all under the surface and be professional. And that's what I have to do now.

Looks can be deceiving in many ways. You never quite know what's going on under the surface. When it comes down to it, we're all actors. We all deceive. Many of us deceive others; sometimes actively, sometimes passively. Most of us deceive only ourselves. When that's the case, how can you possibly know what's true? You end up living a lie.

I don't like getting philosophical. I tend to come out of it with the impression that nothing's real anyway, and that there's no point in even worrying about it.

I think about walking round to the local village pub for a drink or two. It's not something I tend to do often — Megan and I used to pop in every now and again, usually either for a meal every couple of months or a few drinks at Christmas. Neither of us are heavy drinkers. Sometimes I wonder if we should be.

I decide not to. Storming out of the house everytime there's an argument isn't going to do any of us any good — and it'll wear the doormat out pretty sharpish, too.

Sometimes you have to stick these things out, no matter how painful it is. All couples have their ups and downs. We've been having some pretty major downs recently, but there've been ups in the past and I have no doubt we'll have them again. We just need to remember what's important in life.

I've been too bogged down with work, Megan's been too bogged down with Evie. We've drifted slightly because of it. I wonder how much I've used that to my advantage. Some days I imagine she barely notices me leaving the house. I could get away with… Well, you get the picture.

I look out the living room window and decide the car needs a wash. It'll give me something to do — occupy my mind while I calm down — and at least it's productive. Can't beat the 'perfect family man' image, can you?

SIXTEEN

MEGAN

It's now two days since Riley was killed. It's amazing how quickly gossip dies down. I'd like to think if something horrible happened to my child, people would remember it for a bit longer. Perhaps it's one of those situations that 'rocks the community' even though talk has turned to other matters. No doubt there'll be a candlelit vigil within a week. For all the good that'll do.

Mum called again this morning. She hasn't even mentioned it once. It's been all over the national news, never mind locally, but she still hasn't brought it up. Then again, it's not about her or Lauren, nor is it something she can offer advice on, so what's the point? They're the only things she ever opens her mouth for.

Thankfully, she offered to take Evie out today. She said she was heading into town to get some shopping and wouldn't mind a bit of company. I said I wouldn't mind the peace and quiet either.

Chris has gone to speak to the police. He was meant to contact them when he got back yesterday, but he didn't. After the rest of the drama and the argument, he decided he'd wait and go this morning. I don't know how that's going to look for him. But what's done is done.

The cap in the bin has been playing on my mind again. Of course it has. But at the same time I've been trying to force it to the back, knowing I need to believe there's an innocent explanation. I've used distraction as a tool — kept myself busy — but how can you possibly distract yourself from the nagging suspicion that your husband could be a child killer? I think it's the fact that it seems so ridiculous. Chris and I have known each other since we were kids, and he's never said boo to a goose. In a way, that's what worries me the most. If, somehow, it turns out that there's some truth in this, it's going to be even more devastating than it otherwise might have been. Choosing to put my complete faith and trust in Chris leaves me vulnerable to a fall from a great height.

I've taken the opportunity to clean the house from top to bottom. I woke up feeling more energised than I have in recent days, so I thought I might as well take advantage of it. It's been a while since this place has had a proper spring clean, so I don't think August is too late. Half of the cleaning products I got out of the cupboard and onto the kitchen floor have probably long been discontinued, but at least if I use a few of them up it should give us more cupboard space.

In our bedroom, I even decide to hoover inside the

wardrobes. It's difficult in mine, because there are all sorts of things cluttering up the bottom of the wardrobe — shoe boxes, storage cartons and a random carrier bag full of Christmas decorations we bought one year and didn't put up.

Chris is far neater and more organised than I am. He always has been. He has one pair of shoes he wears to work and one pair he wears when he goes out fishing or for walks. The work pair live by the front door, the fishing pair by the back door. I wish my life could be that simple.

His wardrobe is just as clutter-free and organised. There are four suits he wears for work (always taking the suit jacket off the second he arrives at school and just wearing his shirt and tie for the rest of the day, until putting the jacket on again when he leaves) as well as a few casual shirts, three or four t-shirts and a couple of pairs of chinos. It really is about simple living for Chris. I have to drag him out of the house to buy him new clothes once a year, and even then he'll only ever come back with an extra t-shirt or perhaps a tie. As far as he's concerned, he doesn't need much.

I open his wardrobe and poke the hoover around, and it's then that I notice a shoebox tucked away at the back of the wardrobe. Has he secretly bought a third pair of shoes? Shock horror.

I pull the box out and open it. It takes me a few moments to register what's inside, but when I do my blood turns to ice and a cold shiver runs down my spine.

These are drawings and notes, drawn and written by a

young child. Not just any young child, either. They're all named. One's a picture of a man standing in front of a whiteboard, dressed in a suit and tie, with a big beaming smile on his face. *MR MILLER* is written in blue felt-tip pen above him, and the words *BY RILEY* are scrawled at the bottom.

There's more. Short notes, telling Chris he's the 'best teecher in the werld' and 'grait fun'.

As I look through the items in the box, I quickly realise they're all from Riley. There's nothing from any other child. All teachers occasionally bring home things the kids have given them, and Chris is no different — although he hasn't done it for years. This is all from Riley Markham, though. And it's hidden away in a shoebox at the bottom of his wardrobe. Why?

Again, there might be a perfectly innocent explanation, but at the very least it's just *weird*. At the worst... That's not something I want to countenance right now. We should be pulling together as a family, supporting each other and the rest of the community. It's the police who catch killers — no-one else.

A thought crosses my mind. I could ask him about it. After all, it's only a box of drawings and notes. There's nothing incriminating as such. Not in itself. If — *if* — Chris is involved somehow, I'm not going to raise any suspicions by finding this. The cap would be different. Very different.

When I have thoughts like that, I wonder how much trust and faith I really do have in Chris. If I thought there was an innocent explanation, why would I be worried about asking him about the cap?

And that's when I force myself to come to the realisation.

That I believe my husband could be a child killer.

SEVENTEEN

MEGAN

I hear the sound of the front door closing, then Chris kicking off his shoes and walking into the living room.

'How did it go?' I ask. I presume fairly well, seeing as he's back home a few hours later and not banged up in a prison cell somewhere.

'Fine. They wanted to find out more about Riley from a school point of view. Asking about his friends, whether we had any safeguarding concerns over him, all that sort of thing.'

Safeguarding. The thought hadn't even crossed my mind. Could Riley have been killed by an abusive uncle or relative? It must happen all the time.

'And what did you say?'

He shrugs. 'What can I say? He was a normal little boy. Cheeky and cocky from time to time, but I had no concerns.'

'No safeguarding issues?'

'No, nothing.'

I sit down on the arm of the sofa. 'But I don't get why anyone would want to kill him. A little boy of his age can't have any enemies. And if there were no family issues...'

'That we know of,' Chris says. 'You can never be totally sure. You can only ever make a judgement based on what you observe.'

'Like what?'

Chris lets out a huge breath, and I can almost see the tension releasing from his body. 'Just stuff. The sort of things anyone would spot. Comments they make, things they do.'

'Such as?'

He looks at me. 'Why are you so interested?'

I shrug. 'I dunno. It's fascinating, I guess. I don't know anything about it, and you don't talk about work.'

'There's not much to talk about,' he says, looking at his feet.

'So what would the signs be? Have you ever had to investigate anything like that?'

'No, never. Thank God. You're told to look out for abnormal behaviour. Aggression, introversion, overly sexualised behaviour.'

'Overly sexualised?' I ask. 'They're seven years old.'

'Exactly. So displaying sexual knowledge and... well... knowing how it all works. That would be a sign that they've been exposed to something they shouldn't have been.'

This isn't the most pleasant conversation Chris and I have ever had. I wasn't naïve enough to think that teaching was a nice easy job, but I didn't realise they had to get involved with things like that. It makes you wonder why anyone would want to be a teacher.

'Did you get on well with Riley?' I ask.

Chris thinks about this for a moment. 'Yeah, I think so. He was a bit boisterous at times, but nothing out of the ordinary. Nothing I couldn't handle. And he definitely had his sweet side. He was a bit Jekyll and Hyde at times.'

'He quite liked you, didn't he?' I say, my voice squeaking slightly as I push the words out.

'How do you mean?'

'I found the box in the wardrobe. The pictures and notes. He seemed to really admire you as a teacher.'

Chris doesn't respond to this. He just looks at me, his face cold and emotionless.

'What were you doing in there?'

'Cleaning.'

'Inside the shoe box?'

'No, I wondered what it was.'

'It was a box. Which was sealed. In my wardrobe.'

'Don't be silly, Chris. We don't have secrets. It was just—'

'It's not about having secrets!' he bellows. The walls seem to echo with the noise.

'Chris, I—'

'It's about having privacy, Megan.'

'I'm sorry,' I say. 'I just... I wondered why.'

'Why? Why what?'

'Why you brought them home. You don't bring any others home. And after what's happened...'

Chris closes his eyes. I can see his jaw flexing, his teeth grinding. 'All kids draw pictures and write notes to their teachers. Mostly they get kept in a cupboard in the classroom and binned at the end of the year.'

'Except Riley's.'

Chris is silent for a moment. 'I went to the school yesterday. I just needed to be... I don't know. Either I needed the distraction, the return to normality or to be... Well, close to him. I dunno.'

'You went to his parents' house yesterday,' I say.

'Yeah. To. Not in.'

'You didn't speak to them?'

'No.'

'You lied to me.'

'No I didn't, I just didn't want to have to explain why I couldn't go in. I just couldn't, alright? So I went into school and tried to sort through some of last year's crap. And I found the drawings and the notes. I couldn't bring myself to chuck them out. Not this year. Not these ones. So I brought them home. It was almost like keeping a part of him alive.'

I think I can see the glint of a tear beginning to form in Chris's right eye.

'Why couldn't you go into his parents' house?' I ask.

His jaw clenches again. 'I just couldn't.' His voice is tighter than before.

'But why? I don't get it.'

'Because I felt responsible, alright?' he says, rounding on me. His face is inches away from mine, a picture of pain, regret, anger and distress. 'I felt responsible because I was one of the people who was meant to look out for him. If something's happened to him, I should have been in a position to have helped prevent it.'

'But you can't say that, Chris. It could have been a lone weirdo from miles away. Or an accident of some sort. You can't blame yourself.'

'Blame myself?' he yells. 'Jesus Christ, you don't even know the meaning of the word. You just don't *get* it, do you?'

Clearly not, I want to say. 'Then help me understand. What is it? Did you... Did you do something? Were you there? Was it an accident?'

He looks at me, his face showing emotions somewhere between blankness and knowing his life has just changed forever.

He doesn't speak.

'Chris, did you kill Riley Markham?'

I've barely finished the sentence before I feel Chris's hand strike me across the cheek. I stumble backwards, feeling the stinging sensation searing through my jaw. I watch through glassy eyes as Chris walks away.

EIGHTEEN

MEGAN

My backside is starting to feel numb, but I daren't move. I can't move. I've been sitting on the living room floor for over an hour, my knees pulled up tight to my chest, my face resting on them as I cry.

Every conceivable emotion has passed through me. There's been regret — why did I ask him such a stupid question? Why didn't I keep my powder dry? There's anger — my husband has just assaulted me. There's fear — what else is he capable of?

In all the years Chris and I have known each other, we've barely had an argument up until Evie was born. And now this. He isn't the man I knew any more. The Chris I met, the Chris I married, would never have done anything like that in his wildest dreams. Even if he accidentally kicked my foot under the dining table he would be full of apologies, making sure I was alright. It's almost as if the Chris who was standing in this room earlier today is a completely different person.

And if he's now capable of that, what else could he be capable of doing? If he's able to flip so quickly and assault his own wife, what would he do to a young child who antagonised him in some way, or wound him up? It wouldn't have needed to be intentional, or even particularly hard. Riley was only a young lad, after all. Maybe there was a tussle and he slipped. He probably didn't mean to do it. He probably didn't mean to hurt me, or to hit me as hard as he did, but it happened. The red mist just descended and he reacted without thinking. That's not something he's ever done before, and that's what worries me the most.

It's the crushing realisation that I don't know my husband any more. Everything I knew and accepted to be true is now gone. How on earth does someone come to terms with that? That their whole life has been a lie?

My phone buzzes. It takes me a few minutes to look at the screen, mainly because I know deep down this won't be an apology text from Chris. That's not his style, anyway. He'd either apologise in person or just pretend it never happened.

It's Mum, asking when I want her to drop Evie back home. Would it be wrong of me to reply with 'Never'? Right now I just can't handle the thought of it. Then again, it might give me a distraction. I go into the bathroom and look in the mirror, hoping Chris hasn't bruised me. That would take a hell of a lot of explaining to Mum. My face is a little red on that side, but it's nothing that can't be covered up with a bit of foundation and some added blusher on the other cheek.

I tell Mum to come round in half an hour. It's not often I relish the thought of having Mum around too much, but right now I think I'd feel safer. There's no way I can tell her any of the stuff that's happened, but I'm really not sure I can feel secure in the house on my own, nor with Chris around.

What scares me most is that I feel like that. Is Evie safe? If Chris can snap like that with me, he could easily do it with Evie as well. What if she screamed just a little too long, or pinched him just a little too hard?

At the absolute least, if I'm being generous, Chris needs serious help. At the worst, something has changed his entire personality. He's no longer the simple, carefree, loving boy I met and man I married. He's complicated. He's short-tempered. He's violent.

I ask myself if I could have caused this in any way. I know we've drifted apart somewhat since Evie was born, but how much has that affected Chris? It's affected me, but I think that's tempered by how busy I've been with everything else and how insular it's made me. Chris thinks about these things much more. He's sensitive. Does he feel his life starting to crumble away? I don't think so. I hope not. I've tried to make sure that doesn't happen. A number of our friends warned us about it — the baby taking over your life and stopping you from being a couple any more. Slowly, you become two individual parents and not much else.

I wonder whether his more frequent fishing days have had anything to do with it. I've been assuming they're a symptom of whatever's going on in his head, but perhaps they're the cause. Maybe the extra time away from me has made him realise he doesn't need me. But surely he wouldn't feel like that about his own daughter...?

If the truth be told, Chris and Evie probably haven't bonded as well as they should have, either. But that's a huge step from rejecting her completely. All new parents struggle, I'm sure.

And that's when the realisation hits me. I'm making excuses for him. If I'm honest with myself, I've been making excuses for him for a long time. But why? What do I get back? At some point I need to stop, because I don't know what I might find myself excusing. Now I'm trying to excuse domestic violence. The words stick in my throat like bile. The thought of having to use them in the context of my own marriage makes me feel physically sick.

But what else could I be excusing? If I'm honest with myself, I think I know what. It's all starting to piece together and make far more sense than it should. The disappearing acts, the box of pictures, the bloodstained cap. The lifeless body of Riley Markham lying barely a couple of hundred yards from our back door.

And when I start to piece things together in that way, I realise that I've got a whole lot more on my hands than a husband who's going slightly off the rails.

I have a husband who's a killer.

NINETEEN

MEGAN

It's seven o'clock in the evening by the time Chris comes back home. Evie's asleep on my chest. I don't say a word as he enters the living room. I keep my eyes fixed on episode twelve of *Orange is the New Black*. It's not because I don't want to wake Evie up — it's because I can't stand to even look at Chris, never mind speak to him.

He sits down on the sofa on the other side of the room and says nothing for a couple of minutes. I can feel his eyes on me, and for the first time in my life I feel scared in the presence of my own husband. I try not to let it show, though.

Eventually, after what seems like an age, he speaks.

'Do you want a glass of wine?' he says.

I shake my head.

He doesn't speak again for a little while.

'I went for a walk,' he finally says. 'Followed the river

as far as Cottlesford, then cut back through the fields so I'd be back before dark.'

I don't respond in any way. I'm waiting for some sort of apology or at least an acknowledgement, not a running commentary of his fucking walk.

He stands up and walks towards the door. 'I'm going to have a glass even if you're not,' he says.

I close my eyes and try to hold everything in. What the hell is this all about? What's happened to him? I'm desperately trying to cling on to something, giving everything I can to find the most innocent explanation in all this. It feels like I'm standing on the outside, watching someone else's life play out. It's so far removed from the life I knew, I can't handle it. I don't know how to react to anything. What should I be doing? What are the rules? I don't remember any of this being in the manual.

Chris walks back in with his glass of wine and sits back in the same seat. His eyes are on the TV, on a show he's never watched before, rather than even considering trying to explain things to me.

Finally, I break.

'Are we just going to ignore everything that happened earlier?' I ask.

'I'm not ignoring it,' he says.

'It looks like it to me. No apology, no explanation, nothing.'

'Would an apology help?' he asks, not taking his eyes off the screen. 'It wouldn't change anything.'

'Knowing you're sorry would at least do something. There's a reason remorse is a thing.'

'Alright then I'm sorry.' The way he says it means I have no idea whether he's serious or if he's just saying it to placate me. Any little glimpses or snatches of the old Chris seem to be long gone. It's as if I'm speaking to a complete stranger.

'Do you mean that or are you just saying it?' I ask.

His jaw tightens and he closes his eyes. 'Megan, you accused me of murdering a seven-year-old boy.'

'No, I asked you.'

'It's the same thing, whichever way you try and spin it.'

'Chris, I had to ask the question. You've been so weird recently, and then I found the shoebox and the...' I stop myself just in time and trail off. I'm not telling him about the cap. Not yet. I want to hear him say it on his own, without being forced into a corner. That could put both me and Evie in danger.

'The what?' he asks, looking at me.

'The way you've been over the past few weeks. And longer.'

He sighs. 'Megan, I've not been like anything. I've been trying to keep my distance and tread on eggshells because of the way you've been.'

'Me?'

'Come on. Are we going to talk about it or not? We both said before Evie was born that if there were issues afterwards we'd talk about them.'

'What "issues"?' I ask.

'You know what issues. Post-natal depression.'

Even though it's something I've suspected myself, it comes as something of a shock to hear Chris say it. It's one thing trying to deal with something internally, but another thing altogether to realise that someone else has noticed something wrong. Even if there is an aspect of that, post-natal depression doesn't put blood-stained caps in your wheelie bin or make local children turn up dead. It's a distraction tactic from Chris, trying to change the subject, attempting to shift the blame for the impending collapse of our marriage.

'Look at the facts,' he says. 'Your mood is low. You're seeing negatives everywhere. A child in my class dies and I bring home a couple of mementoes to remember him by, and you jump to the conclusion that I've killed him. You've barely left the house since Evie was born, you've stopped communicating with our friends. Megs, you know the checklist as well as I do. Is it really worth risking our marriage over it?'

Right now, I don't know the answer to that question. But I play along all the same.

'I'm not going to take any tablets,' I say. I need to be able to think clearly at all times. I'm not about to let myself be gaslighted.

'Fine. But speak to the doctor. I'm sure there are lots of ways of dealing with it and getting better. It's not all about drugs. Most doctors are trying to help people in other ways now. Talking therapies, mind exercises. All that stuff.'

Great. A shrink. The worst thing is that I know Chris isn't wrong. I know I'm struggling. I know, medically speaking, it's probably post-natal depression. But I also know that right now that isn't the biggest problem in my life or the biggest problem facing our marriage. Something inside, though, tells me I do need to get help. At the very least, if I can rule my own muddled mind out as a cause for what I now believe to be true, I'll be one step closer to knowing what's really going on.

'Alright,' I say. 'I'll ring them in the morning.'

TWENTY

MEGAN

Sitting in this waiting room always brings back painful memories. People aren't often in doctors' waiting rooms for happy reasons, but the occasions that seem to stand out in my mind are the times we visited when we couldn't conceive. Of course, that particular issue seemed to resolve itself, but it's a time in my life I'd still rather forget.

I wonder how much of it affected me on a psychological level. I'd come to terms with the fact I was never going to have children, and then we miraculously ended up expecting Evie. I was delighted. Of course I was. We both were. But it's a hell of a lot to come to terms with.

It was all we'd ever wanted, and everyone told us it would be a rough ride. They were right. We believed them, but we massively underestimated how hard it would be.

The guilt was the worst thing. Feeling so completely dreadful for occasionally wishing we didn't have her. Praying for just one full night of sleep, or to be able to go out and see a film together. Like we used to.

I wonder if that contributed to the way I feel about things now. To want something so badly and have to come to terms with the fact that you can't have it, then to be given it, enjoy all the happiness it brings and then realise that it wasn't so great after all — that's got to take its toll.

I don't know how long I'm in my daydream for, but I'm jolted back into the room by the gentle *ding* of the screen displaying my name, telling me to head to Doctor Ashford's office.

Doctor Ashford's a pleasant enough guy. Genial when you need him to be, but he's always honest. Brutally honest, at times. He was very understanding when we saw him about the fertility issues, which was why I specifically asked to see him today. He reminds me a little of the actor, Richard Griffiths. I imagine if he grew a beard, he'd be able to do a fantastic turn as Santa Claus.

'So how are you?' he asks, as I take off my jacket and put it over the back of the chair.

I don't know why doctors always ask that. The answer is, quite obviously, 'not great', seeing as I'm sufficiently unwell to have made a doctor's appointment. But it's all an irrelevance, because we're British, so the answer is always 'not bad'.

'Not bad,' I say, sitting down on the chair. 'But not great either, if I'm honest.'

Doctor Ashford looks at me and smiles, willing me to tell him more.

'I don't really know what it is I'm here for. Well, I do. But I don't know if it's daft or if I'm just being silly or what.'

He smiles again. He must get a lot of this. So many of us are rubbish at speaking to doctors or admitting something's wrong.

'Is it something physical?' he asks.

'Not really, no.'

He nods. 'Can you describe how you feel?'

I sigh. 'I think it's some sort of post-natal depression.'

'PPD, we call it. Postpartum depression. But it's essentially the same thing. What makes you think that's what you have? Can you describe the symptoms you have for me?'

I take a deep breath. 'Tiredness. Irritability. I don't feel like I'm able to connect with my daughter. I just feel... totally wiped out. And kind of paranoid about stuff.'

'What sort of stuff?'

I think for a moment. Should I tell him I'm so loopy I've become paranoid my husband is a murderer? Of course I should. He's a medical professional. He needs to know the full facts in order to help me.

I look at the floor. 'Oh. All sorts, really. Nothing specific.' I force a smile, but inside I'm kicking myself for not saying the words.

'I understand. Having a baby is a huge thing. It takes an enormous toll on your body and on your mind. Is there any history of depression or mental illness in your family?'

I shake my head. 'No. None.'

'Any family history of drug use or childbirth complications?'

'Not that I'm aware of.' The thought of my mother getting smacked off her tits on heroin elicits a small smile from me, which the doctor thankfully doesn't notice.

'I notice your daughter isn't with you today. Is she with her dad?'

'No, she's with my mum. She looks after her a couple of days a week so I can get things done.'

He smiles. 'I see. And your symptoms. Have they got any better? Worse? Stayed the same?'

It sounds strange, but that's actually a difficult question to answer. 'Stayed the same, I guess. Overall, I mean. Some days are worse than others.'

'And how do you cope when you have really bad days?'

'I don't. Not really. I mean, I push on and get through it, but the whole time I'm just dying inside.' I feel tears starting to well up, so I stop talking. I'm not a cryer. Never have been. And I don't want to start now.

Doctor Ashford turns away from me for a moment and types a few notes on his computer. I don't know if he does so because he sensed I was about to become emotional, but I'm thankful to him all the same.

'And what about thoughts?' he says. 'Have you had any dark or destructive thoughts? Any fantasies of harm, anything like that?'

I swallow. Hard. *Yes, I've become obsessed with the idea that my husband's a child murderer* I scream inside my head, but what comes out of my mouth is 'No'.

'And are you breastfeeding?'

'Sort of,' I say. 'Evie's not great at feeding, but I tend to express and feed her from the bottle. It's still breast milk.'

'Okay. I'm not going to prescribe any medication, for a couple of reasons. Partly because of the breastfeeding. Any medication you take will pass on to your baby through your milk. Plus, many of these drugs do tend to make things a bit worse in the short-term, and some can even bring on thoughts of suicide or self-harm, which obviously isn't something we want to happen. So I think we're better off pursuing other avenues at the moment.'

'Do you think it is post-natal depression, then?' I ask.

'Postpartum depression. And I don't know. I'm personally very careful about diagnosing things like that. I'm not the sort of doctor who dishes out drugs like they're Smarties, and I know myself how physically and mentally draining having children can be. Believe me, it doesn't stop once they're walking, either. My eldest's currently badgering me for thousands a year to go to uni and study Japanese art. I doubt we'll ever see that money again if that's his chosen career path,' he says, laughing. Some people might think that insensitive, but I actually quite like it. It's just his way of putting himself on a level with his patients.

'But what else could it be?'

Doctor Ashford raises his eyebrows and sighs. 'It could be any number of things. Personally, I think PPD is over-diagnosed. If you look at the symptoms,' he says counting them off on his fingers. 'Lethargy, anxiety, changes to sleeping patterns, irritability, eating less than you used to... They're all symptoms of having children, full-stop. Have you tried getting more exercise?'

I wasn't expecting him to say that, and I'm fairly sure my face tells him so, as he immediately tries to clarify what he meant.

'Increased exercise can release more serotonin and dopamine, which are what many people refer to as "feel-good hormones". Low serotonin levels can contribute heavily to symptoms of depression and anxiety.'

I wonder for a moment if he might have a point. Before I fell pregnant with Evie, I used to get quite a lot of exercise. I was the county cross-country champion for three years, and used to go on regular runs. Then I fell pregnant and stopped. The advice the NHS gives is not to make any drastic changes when you fall pregnant. Don't suddenly start exercising, but don't make any changes to your regular patterns either. Somehow, though, going on long runs with an unborn baby bouncing around inside me just didn't feel right. I wanted to stay at home and do all I could to keep the baby safe, especially after all we'd been through to get that far.

'It sounds ideal,' I say, 'but I don't know how I'm going to get the time to do that. I barely even get time to brush my own teeth, never mind introduce a new exercise regime.'

'Are you working at the moment?' he asks. 'I noticed you mentioned earlier that your mum takes your daughter for a couple of days a week.'

'She does, but that barely gives me enough time to catch up on housework and tidying. I could get up an hour earlier and go for a run, like I used to years ago, but at the moment every second of sleep is like gold dust to me.'

'Well, there are other things we can do. But personally I'd recommend trying to get out of the house more. Walk to places instead of driving — that can give you huge health benefits, both mentally and physically. Just getting outside and getting some fresh air can do wonders. It's all too easy to get cooped up in your own house for weeks when you have a baby. Even a ten-minute walk around the block can do you the world of good.'

'I'll give it a go,' I say, although I don't feel hopeful. I should, though. Because I know he's right. I don't need drugs. I just need to be able to drag myself off my backside and do this for myself — and for Evie.

I think for a moment about telling him that actually I *have* been having dangerous thoughts, but something tells me not to. Because they aren't just thoughts, are they? I don't *think* I saw a bloodstained cap in our wheelie bin, and I don't *think* Chris hid a secret stash of mementoes from Riley Markham. I know both of those things are true. The only thing I don't know for certain is what those two things mean, but I do know I'm going to need to have a clear head if I'm ever going to get to the truth.

TWENTY-ONE

Kai Bolton always used to look forward to Tuesdays and Thursdays. Those were the days he got to see his dad.

He still didn't quite understand why Dad didn't live with them any more. All he'd been told was that Dad was moving out and Uncle Tony was moving in. Mum and Dad didn't like each other very much. He'd worked that much out. He wasn't a kid any more. He was nine.

Mum used to moan at Dad all the time when he was still living with them. She used to call him lazy and useless, as well as some other words he couldn't remember and some that'd got him in trouble for using at school. Dad wasn't happy for *ages,* but now he was a lot better because he had Angela. Mum said he wasn't allowed to call her Auntie Angela, and that was fine with him. He didn't like Angela. She had a face that looked a bit like a walnut, and her boobies were way too big.

Mum used to drop Kai over at his dad's house on

Tuesday and Thursday mornings whenever it was the school holidays. Mum went to work on Tuesdays and Thursdays and the strict man in the suit said he had to spend at least one day a week with Dad. When it was school time, it was usually a Saturday or a Sunday, but that was rubbish because then he didn't get to go to the football with Uncle Tony. Or just Tony, as his mum said he should call him. The school holidays were better. At the end of each Tuesday and Thursday, Dad would drive him back home again. It had to be at four o'clock, though, as Dad had to go somewhere after that. He never told Kai where, but Kai guessed it must be somewhere important. Mum got home from work at half past four, and Tony would be home just before seven o'clock, but Mum said Kai was a big boy now and he could wait for half an hour on his own as long as he stayed in the living room and watched TV and didn't go into the kitchen.

Mum was always worried about the kitchen. She said it had lots of sharp things and appliances that could hurt Kai. But Kai wasn't stupid. He was nine now.

At nine, you're big enough to do all sorts of things. Including going in the kitchen. But it was better to keep Mum happy than to annoy her. At nine, you're big enough to walk home on your own too. That's what Dad had been telling him for the past few weeks. He told Kai not to tell Mum, though, because she wouldn't be happy. She still thought he was a baby, and if she found out Kai was walking home from his Dad's house she'd go mental and never let him go out again. Kai didn't like the sound of that, so he decided to keep quiet.

Walking home on his own was alright, though. He actually quite liked it. It made him feel older, and anyway it wasn't that far from Dad's house to his own house. You could go the long way round by the road or you could cut through the park and down by the river. That was a lot quicker, and you didn't see so many people, but Mum would go *extra* mental if she knew he was walking by the river on his own, especially after what happened to that little boy a few weeks ago.

Whenever he walked down here with his Mum she'd always walk by the water and make sure he was on the other side of her, even though he liked walking close to the water. It was stupid. The water wasn't even deep. It probably wouldn't even come up to his knees.

All mums worried, though. His mates all said the same thing. Apart from Finlay Keane's mum. Finlay Keane's mum was *really* cool. She let them play Nerf guns *inside* the house. Kai's mum wouldn't even let him have a Nerf gun, and the other boys' mums sometimes let them play them but only outside in the garden. Finlay's mum and dad have a massive house though so it wouldn't really matter because their house is bigger than most people's gardens. Plus their garden has that fake grass stuff in it so technically it's more like a carpet and the inside of the house is more like the outside. Kai thought people were weird.

He stopped and looked into the river. He always liked

this bit. The water flowed really fast here, and you could see all the pebbles underneath, with the water splitting as it washed over them. He didn't know how long he stood there watching the water washing over the pebbles, but before he knew what was happening, his legs were dangling a few inches off the floor as the arm crushed his windpipe and lifted him in the air. He tried to scream or call out, but he couldn't. He couldn't get the air from his lungs to his mouth, and instead just made a horrible gurgling noise which sounded like his Mum pulling the plug out of the bath.

He tried kicking at whoever was holding him, but he was starting to lose strength in his legs. He felt something rough around his neck — something that scratched and burned a bit. The arm started to let go of him, but he still couldn't breathe. He landed on his knees on the edge of the river, and brought his hands up to his throat. There was some rope or something tied around his neck. He could hear the blood pulsing in his eardrums, bursting to try and get through the blood vessels but the rope was too tight. It felt like his head was going to burst. His lips hurt. He could see stuff at the edges of his eyes. It was starting to go dark. Just before it went completely dark, he felt a sharp pain in the back of his head. The last thing Kai saw was the splashes of blood hitting the pebbles, the red liquid marbling in the water as it flowed away downstream.

TWENTY-TWO

CHRIS

I feel dirty. As soon as it happens I get a huge burst of excitement and feel as if I'm on top of the world, but that feeling quickly dissipates and turns into a sense that I'm the worst person in the world. It's incredible how quickly that feeling changes. I don't know what makes me keep doing it. I know it's wrong. I know how many lives I'm ruining. I know family units will be smashed apart. But it's like feeding an addiction.

I'm fairly sure I remember reading somewhere that this is how addictions manifest themselves. It's that yearning to feel that rush of excitement again, to try and better it. The problem is, the more you do it the less you enjoy it, so the more you need to do it to get the rush. It's a devastating, never-ending spiral.

If it's an addiction, I guess this is the hangover. The 'I'm never drinking again' bit. But we all know that's bullshit. After a day or so, none of us can resist that sweet nectar. It's much the same for me, although my new addiction isn't alcohol.

I've never been the sort to have an addictive personality. Up to now. In many ways, it makes me realise what I've been missing all this time. Some people might call it a mid-life crisis, but then again I've never really been one to care about what people think. To me, it's confirmation that I've been living a sheltered life for far too long.

But that's not how I feel right this second. Right now, I feel like my whole world is about to close in on me. Like I'm about to get found out. Megan suspects something. I know she does. She's been acting even weirder than usual lately, and I'm waiting for the day when she asks me outright. What would I say? It sounds ridiculous, but I really don't know. It's one thing keeping things from her and just not telling her, but it's another thing entirely to lie outright to her face. Having said that, though, the truth isn't an option.

If I said yes, that would be the end of us. It'd be the end of me. It would be the end of my career and my life as I know it. Having to lie to Megan would be a whole new step. Not that I haven't been surprised enough recently at the things I never thought I was capable of doing. I guess life is a constant learning curve.

I don't know about other people, but I tend to get the feeling that nothing is ever complete. I'm always discovering new things about myself. It's just that, until recently, I never did anything about them. I was quite happy plodding along in my own bubble, oblivious to everything.

Megan was in when I got home. She didn't say much, which was something of a relief. The hardest thing would be looking her in the eye so soon after what I'd done. Instead, I went upstairs and scrubbed my hands in the sink before showering, trying to get every last trace of it off me.

When I was a kid I used to think that people could see what I was thinking. Over time, I trained myself not to think anything that was even slightly out of the ordinary, for fear that other people would be able to read my thoughts and judge me. Those same feelings are creeping back now. Can people smell sin?

As I use up half a bottle of shower gel and scrub my skin red raw, I know I need to put a stop to this somehow. All I'm doing is hurting people. It needs to stop.

But, deep down, I know I can't. This is who I am now. I can't go back, can't take back the things I've done. And all the while I can feel that new part of me growing, building in confidence as the old me starts to wither away into the background like a fading flower.

I look down at my hands as the water runs down my arms and cascades off my fingertips. They look like someone else's hands. I'm standing in the comfort of my own shower, in my own home, knowing what these hands were doing just half an hour or so earlier. The dichotomy makes my head spin. It's like looking back at the memory of a film or TV programme. My brain can't quite reconcile that it was me doing those things. Maybe there's a reason for that. Perhaps this is how people get away with it — their brains detach from the reality in an attempt to bridge the gap of cognitive dissonance.

Now we're getting philosophical, aren't we? Now we're getting heavy. But what's philosophical about it? When you lay it out in the open, it's a dirty act — something everyone instinctively knows to be wrong. It's something that can shatter families forever. Yet it still keeps happening. It's an itch that certain people still feel the unbearable need to scratch. Will that ever end? I doubt it. Somewhere, it's carved deep into the human psyche.

I know it can't carry on, though. It just can't. Sooner or later, you'll always get found out. It's a matter of time, quitting while you're ahead.

Sometimes I wonder whether it's the getting caught that would devastate me the most or the realisation of what I'd done. I like to think it would be the latter, but I wouldn't put money on it. After all, I know what I've done is wrong. There's no doubting that. But it still doesn't stop me. Why?

I guess a psychologist would say it's because I see myself as being above morality. I know that's not true, though. It's because I can't get enough of it. Because it *is* an addiction. Because the high is so intense it just can't be topped by anything else — anything moral.

And, like most addicts, I wish I'd never tasted the first drop.

TWENTY-THREE

MEGAN

I watch through the kitchen window as Chris wrestles with an old tree stump towards the bottom of the garden. He's been talking for months about taking it out, but for some reason he seems to have chosen now as the time to do it.

As I rinse the washing up suds off my hands, I can hear the faint sound of Chris's phone ringing. I know it's Chris's phone, because his ringtone is the theme tune from the *Star Wars* films. I head upstairs to see if I can find it — he's obviously switched his voicemail off, because the phone just rings and rings.

I finally find it under a pile of clothes on the bed. I pick it up and look at the screen. It's Rebecca Atkinson-West, the headteacher at St Bartholomew's, where Chris works. I answer the call.

'Oh, is that Megan?' she says, in a tone of voice which sounds disappointed and disapproving. I'm not sure how the woman does it, but she somehow manages to make everything sound condescending. Chris says she's alright, and I'm sure she's fine as a headteacher, but she's not the sort of person I'd like to spend much time with.

'Yes, he left his phone here. Sorry. Can I take a message?'

'I really should speak to him directly,' she says, and I get the sense that perhaps this isn't just her being patronising; it actually sounds like quite a serious moment. But how many things can be that serious that the headteacher would phone a staff member in the middle of the school holidays? Unless... Unless it's connected to Riley Markham.

'The only problem is I don't know when he's going to be back in,' I say. I'm not technically lying; I'm just choosing not to add the detail about Chris only being in the back garden.

Rebecca sounds conflicted 'Ah. Well, I suppose it's probably best if you can pass the message on to him as quickly as possible. I really should speak to him directly, but the news will only get to him some other way. I guess it would be better if it came from you.'

Gee, thanks, I want to say. 'If what came from me?'

I hear Rebecca sighing on the other end of the phone. When she speaks, her voice sounds frailer than usual. I don't know if it's fear, panic or what, but it concerns me.

What she says concerns me even more.

'The police have found another body. It's another one of our pupils. A young boy.'

My breath catches in my throat and I don't know what to say.

'Oh god,' I finally manage. 'Who?'

'You mustn't breathe a word of this to anyone until the family have been told, Megan. You have to promise me. Chris will need to know, but it's not public information yet.'

'Alright. I promise.' I can only imagine the pain it would bring to the boy's family to hear of his death via Facebook or a WhatsApp group, rather than from the police.

'His name was Kai Bolton,' she says.

'Was he in Chris's class?'

'Not this past year, no. A couple of years ago.'

'What happened?'

She takes a moment to compose herself. 'They're not sure yet. I imagine probably a few things, but they won't tell us anything until they've investigated further.'

'Was he… a good kid?' Even though I've never even heard Kai's name before, for some reason I want to know all about him. I feel I need to get to know these children, especially if…

'He had a bit of a troubled background. Nothing serious in the grand scheme of things, but definitely a broken family by local standards. He was in trouble more often than not, but… Well, no child deserves this, do they?' For a few moments, I detect a heavy hint of sadness in Rebecca's voice. I've never known her to show any sort of emotion at all, so this all feels quite alien.

'I'll let him know. Kai Bolton?' I say, confirming his name, although I know I'm never likely to forget it. It's now indelibly printed on my mind, and always will be.

'Yes. Thank you, Megan. Tell Chris if he needs to call me, he can do. Any time. Day or night.'

'I will. Thanks.'

I end the phone call and put Chris's mobile back down on the bed in front of me. I look across it and out through our bedroom window to the rolling fields and treetops beyond. The thought of two young boys having met their deaths here in recent days is absolutely devastating. I try to imagine how I would feel if it was my own son — the son I never had — but I can't. Maybe it's my brain protecting me, knowing the thought would be too painful.

'Alright?'

Chris's voice startles me and shocks me back into the here and now. I spin around and he looks at me quizzically.

'What's wrong?' he asks.

My eyes inadvertently flick towards his mobile phone, and his gaze slowly carries over towards it. He looks at the phone for a couple of seconds before looking back at me.

'What have you been doing?' he says.

'Nothing. Your phone rang.'

I see him swallow, his Adam's apple bobbing up and down in his throat.

'Who was it,' he says, more as a statement than a question.

'Rebecca. She called because she has some news.'

'About Riley?'

'Sort of.' There are so many thoughts going through my mind, I don't know what to think. I just want to scream and throw myself out of the window, but that isn't going to do me any good. 'She said the police had found another body. Another boy from the school.'

Chris just looks at me, his face not changing in the slightest. Gradually, he starts to drain of all colour and his eyelids begin to flicker.

'Who?' he asks, almost whispering, after what seems like an age.

'A boy called Kai Bolton.'

He nods slowly. 'Where was he found?'

'She didn't say. I didn't ask. But she said you can call her any time of the day or night. She wanted to make sure you found out either through me or through her before anyone else tells you.'

He nods again, then sits on the bed before lying down on his side, bringing his knees up to his chest and letting out the most pained, agonising sobs I've ever heard anyone make.

TWENTY-FOUR

MEGAN

I held Chris for almost half an hour. I've never seen a grown man cry himself to sleep, never mind in broad daylight. I don't imagine he's been getting much sleep at night these past few days, even though he'd never say so himself.

All that was going through my mind as I held him was how could I possibly have thought he was a killer? I know this man like nobody else, and I could see how he'd responded to the news of Kai's death. That's not the sort of act someone can just put on. Is it?

Chris finds it difficult enough not to tell me what he's got me for my birthday. I can't imagine for one moment he'd be able to keep a secret as huge as this. But knowing all that still doesn't stop the gnawing, bugging feeling in my gut. The voice that shouts out loud *Something isn't right*.

I've read the same news articles and true crime books

as most other people. I know how it goes. All the friends and family say 'I had no idea they were capable of something like that!' or 'But he seemed so normal!'.

Chris is still asleep upstairs, and Evie is playing with her toys in the living room. I watch her as she picks them up and throws them back down, or practises bashing them together. It's not really playing as we know it, but she's learning what to do.

For some unknown reason that really rankles with me, we have to have the TV on in the background. It doesn't matter what programme, and there doesn't need to be any sound, but the moving pictures alone seem to keep Evie calm.

Right now, the TV is tuned to *BBC News 24*. I wanted to watch, to see what was being said about Riley and Kai, to try and find out more about the sort of act that could break apart a community and countless families.

From what I can make out in the silence, there's some sort of political meeting going on in Brussels, and we keep seeing the same shot of the Prime Minister walking up a path towards a large white door, smiling as she enters.

And then I see it at the bottom of the screen. It's the name of our village that catches my eye and, being the last word in the headline, it takes a minute or so before it scrolls back round again. Every word is one I'll never forget.

And there it is, the twenty-four-hour rolling news letting the nation and the world know that a second young child has been found dead in our village. There's no mention of his name, so I can only presume that not all friends and family have been told yet. It's only right they don't find out this way, but it will have the unintentional effect of making every other person in the area panic that it could be a member of their family.

The camera cuts back to the studio, and I unmute the TV. I have a feeling the subject's about to move on to the latest killing. I'm right.

'—a second child's body,' the newsreader says, leaving me to piece together the first half of the sentence for myself. 'Police say they are not yet ready to name the victim, nor have they commented on any connection between this and the murder of seven-year-old Riley Markham last week, whose body was found less than three hundred yards from the site of this most recent incident. Lisa Rhodes reports.'

The image on the screen changes to one that I instantly recognise. It's the stream that runs near our house. The stream I often walk down with Chris and Evie. A place I know like the back of my hand. A place I'll never be able to walk again.

'A quiet, quintessential English village. And now home to two brutal killings of young children,' the reporter begins, making me angry at the way she's portraying our community. 'Although police have been reticent to link this most recent discovery with the death of another young boy just last week, it's clear that local residents are deeply concerned about the events in their village.'

The shot cuts to a replayed interview of a man with a beard, whom I don't recognise. 'It's just terrible. Dreadful,' he says, before mentioning the fact that he walks his dogs along the river every day and couldn't imagine such a thing happening here.

Then the camera switches to one of the mums I recognise from the village. I don't recall her name, but I know her son is Daniel Crawford. Chris has told me all about Daniel. She holds her son close to her hip as she tells the off-camera reporter 'I don't feel safe down here any more. Definitely not. I know the police aren't making the link yet, but everyone else is.'

'It's clear that this is a small village community shocked to its core,' the reporter says, now in full view as she holds a microphone up in front of her mouth. 'Locals tell me it's one of the last places of its kind in Britain — the sort of village where you feel safe leaving your doors unlocked, where everyone knows each other. This, for them, has been a brutal reminder of what lurks in the modern world,' she says, talking as if we're some sort of third-world redneck backwater. 'For now, though, the focus is on finding the killer or killers of these two innocent young boys, and ensuring they're brought to justice.'

And, just like that, the news moves on to the England cricket team's latest collapse against the West Indies. As if everything that was just said is irrelevant.

I sit for a few moments, watching the screen. Evie makes a half-chuckling half-gurgling noise, and I force a smile for her. I pick her up and carry her on my hip through to the kitchen. She protests, but it's tough. I've got things to do. I need to occupy my mind before I go crazy.

I put her in the doorway bouncer in the bedroom, and she soon stops complaining. Instead, she bounces up and down quite happily. At least I know she can't get into any mischief here.

The sun starts to stream in through the window. It won't be long before the sun goes down. I really should think about putting Evie to bed, but I'm desperate for the loo.

I keep the door open. I can see Evie in the doorway bouncer from here and, more importantly, she can see me.

When I'm finished, I turn on the hot tap, ready to wash my hands, but freeze. I turn the tap off and look more closely. My heart jumps when I realise what I'm looking at.

There are bloodstains in the sink. It looks as though someone's done a half decent job of clearing up after themselves, but there are spots and splashes on the side of the sink that have been missed. They're streaked with water, as if someone has been desperately trying to scrub blood from their hands.

I look over at Evie, with her huge beaming smile. But all I see is a killer's genes looking back at me.

TWENTY-FIVE

LAST YEAR

Chris squeezes my hand as I try to get into position, the blue paper tearing underneath me as my body squirms.

'Just lie back and get yourself comfortable,' the sonographer says. 'I'm going to put this gel on your tummy. It'll probably be a bit cold, so I apologise for that.'

Everything's cold at the moment. Summer is well and truly gone, and I've come to the realisation that I don't have any jumpers that will fit my growing belly. I'm certainly not going to spend a load of money on clothes I'll only be wearing for a few weeks, though.

'You might already be aware, but at this scan we're going to have a look at baby's internal organs and see how the growth is going. There's a chance we might also be able to determine the sex. It's very usual that we can't tell, depending on how baby's positioned, but would you like to know the sex if I'm able to see?'

I look at Chris, and he looks at me.

'Yes,' I say. 'Yes please,' ignoring the personal dislike I have for medical professionals referring to 'baby' rather than 'the baby' or 'your baby', as if it's the poor bugger's name.

The sonographer moves the scanner over my belly, and begins to push and prod. That's one thing they never show you on TV — how bloody hard these people shove the scanner into you during an ultrasound. I yelp a couple of times, partly through my own pain but also because I'm worried she's going to hurt the baby.

'It's alright. She knows what she's doing,' Chris says, as if he can read my mind. I often think he can.

'Okay, there we go,' the sonographer says. 'Baby's in a good position. I'm just having a look at the mouth and nose area now. That all looks fine. No signs of a cleft palate. Spine looks good, too. I'm just going to see if I can encourage baby to turn over now and get a look at the chest area.'

She pokes and prods me even more, and I bite my lip to stop myself yelping in pain.

'There we go. Can you see that there? That's baby's heart. You can see all four chambers here, look.'

I look through misty eyes. She's right. I can quite clearly see the internal workings of my baby's heart. It's absolutely incredible. Just seeing my baby is one thing, but being able to see inside its body is a minor miracle.

She pokes around a bit more, checking the baby's

kidneys and other internal organs, and makes lots of reassuring comments.

'Baby looks absolutely fine,' she says. 'Very healthy. You must be doing all the right things.'

Chris lets out a small laugh, and I know exactly what he's thinking. I've already filled a bookcase with every pregnancy and baby book I could find in Waterstone's, and I've digested every word on every page. After what we went through to try and have a child in the first place, I'm not about to take even the smallest risk now.

'I hope so,' I say, hearing my voice cracking ever so slightly.

'So do you want to know the sex of the baby?' the sonographer says again.

I don't need to look at Chris this time. We both agreed from the start — from before I was even pregnant — that we would want to know the gender. It would allow us to prepare, mentally more than anything, and would make everything more real. As strange as it sounds, even with a small person growing inside me, it still hasn't really hit home that we're going to be parents, that in a few weeks from now we'll be solely responsible for a tiny baby. Our child.

I've always said I'd be happy with a boy or a girl. To me, all children are precious and we've waited so long I really couldn't care — as long as the baby is happy and healthy. But Chris's family are more traditional. They've always put more stock in the boys. 'The paternal line' as Chris's dad always used to call it.

They've got a tradition of passing the father's name down and using it as the first-born son's middle name. I think that's sweet, and we've talked about the possibility of doing that if we have a boy. The sense I got from Chris was almost the expectation that it *would* be a boy. I've always imagined us having a boy, too. Lots of our friends have young boys and whenever I think of my baby, it's a boy I imagine. I don't know if that means anything. Probably not. Maybe it's a mother's intuition, at best.

Chris has always been great with his nephews. He takes them to the park to play football, and buys them the best Christmas presents. He always seems to know exactly what little boys want — remote-controlled helicopters, robot dogs, the lot. He manages to pitch it just right, and every year seems to win the unspoken Best Uncle award.

With his nieces, though, he seems clueless. 'I don't know anything about little girls,' he always says, before making a joke of it. 'I haven't been one yet.' He might joke, but I think it's actually quite sad to witness the fact that he can't bond with his nieces as well as he can with his nephews. It's as if his relationship with them is missing something.

'Yes. If you're able to tell,' I say to the sonographer.

'These things are never one hundred percent certain,' she says, 'but I've been doing this for a long time and I've not been wrong yet. Besides which, I wouldn't tell you if I wasn't as sure as I could be.'

I look at Chris and smile. We're about to find out the

sex of our baby. The child that we're going to bring into the world, love and nurture until the day we die. The completion of our family. Our son.

'It's a girl,' the sonographer says, and I see Chris's smile begin to fall away.

TWENTY-SIX

MEGAN

I've seen that face many times when I fall asleep. It's haunted me ever since that day. Of course, Chris said he didn't mind whether we had a boy or a girl, and claimed that he was just surprised when the sonographer told us we were having a girl.

I scrutinised his face when Evie was born. I should have been more focused on her, but all that was going through my mind was that Chris was going to be disappointed. That he was going to reject our child. That he was going to resent me for not providing him with a son.

I sometimes wonder if that's why I've had my own problems bonding with Evie. Perhaps I've been too focused on keeping Chris happy and making sure he wasn't genuinely disappointed with our daughter, I've let my own care for her slip.

To give him his dues, he's never given me any sort of

indication of disappointment or regret. He's shown nothing but love for Evie — despite the bonding issues — and I know I have to trust in that.

But my mind won't stop niggling.

I wonder if this has all been some sort of 'revenge psychosis' — if there even is such a thing. Has he been so unable to cope with not being able to have a son that he has felt the need to deprive others of theirs? The thought sounds ridiculous, but I'm well aware of how fragile a person's mind can be — particularly when under situations of great stress.

All I can keep doing is putting myself in his shoes. Trying to think like him. To have dreamed about having a son for so long, to think he was unable to have any children, then to be presented not only with a daughter, but a wife who was almost completely unable to look after her. He's had to deal with my own issues after the birth of Evie. It's been a huge amount to have on his shoulders, and I don't think anyone could blame him for being mentally fragile.

But it's a huge, enormous leap from mentally fragile to crazed serial killer. My logical mind just can't make that jump, and in many ways I'm thankful for that. I don't want to think that about my husband. Who does?

It's the sort of thing you read in books and see in films. But it's reality too, isn't it? It's believed that Harold Shipman — Britain's most prolific serial killer — murdered his hundreds of elderly victims because they reminded him of his own mother. And everyone said the same about him. *He seemed so nice. I never would have thought that about him.* I guess it's only natural. If serial killers walked around with crazed looks on their faces, wielding their bloody axes above their heads in the middle of Tesco, they wouldn't last very long. It's sheer self-preservation to look and act normal, to blend in.

Everything is starting to make sense. The pieces of the puzzle are beginning to fall into place. Motive, means and opportunity. That's what they need, isn't it? Well, now we've got all three. He had the opportunity — he was out fishing when Riley Markham was killed and I was at the doctor's when Kai Bolton died. Chris could have been anywhere. Did he go out for half an hour or so? The means doesn't even need questioning. He's a grown man, and not a small one at that. Riley and Kai were both young boys. Chris could have overpowered them more than easily. And then there's that motive. Is this all because we weren't able to have a son? Because Evie was a girl? Is this my fault?

My mind's running away with me again, but does he resent me for not being able to provide him with a son? Does that mean I'm next? Will I be his last victim? And what about Evie?

I can't even remember which way round the biology goes. Is it the sperm or the egg that determines the gender of the baby? Chris would know. He's the teacher. So does that mean it's either him or me that will end up dead too? How many more children need to die before that happens?

I can feel my breath increasing and I try to stave off the inevitable panic attack. I need to speak to someone about this. I have to. It's insane trying to keep something like this to myself. But who can I tell? I don't have any close friends. I can't bring the subject up with Chris. Mum would tell everyone within a five-hundred-mile radius.

As ever, I'm completely on my own.

I could speak to Doctor Ashford. Wouldn't he be legally bound by patient-doctor confidentiality? He wouldn't be able to tell anyone what we discussed, would he? I'm fairly sure there's a clause that says doctors are allowed to disclose things if they think a law has been broken, or people's lives are in danger. This situation covers both of those.

But I don't think I want Doctor Ashford to listen to me as a friend, to tell me I'm being unreasonable or talk through the situation with me. I want him to tell me these are paranoid delusions. To prove that the cap never existed — that I imagined it. That being at home on my own all the time is making my mind play tricks on me.

I guess it's not often someone wants to be told they're going mad, but right now I want that more than anything else in the world. What will they do? Put me on medication? Suggest I go somewhere for a few weeks to get my mind straight? Then what will happen to Evie? Either way, it's got to be preferable to the alternative. It's far better she's left with her dad for a bit while Mummy gets better than it would being left with a killer. And that's why I hope beyond hope that this is all in my mind. That I'm imagining things.

I call the doctor's surgery to make an appointment. They tell me there's nothing left for today and in any case Doctor Ashford isn't in. The receptionist says I'll have to call again tomorrow to make an appointment for then. I tell her it's urgent, that it's related to what I came to see him about last time and that I really need to see Doctor Ashford first thing in the morning. She tells me if it's urgent I should call NHS Direct or go to a hospital. I tell her again it's Doctor Ashford I need to see. I say he'll understand. Finally, she relents and books me in for nine o'clock tomorrow morning.

Evie gurgles and smacks her hand on the tray of her high chair, over and over.

'You okay to stay there for a minute, sweetie?' I say, knowing damn well she's not capable of answering me. I open the kitchen door and step out into the garden. I stand staring at the wheelie bin, the movement of Evie hammering the tray of her high chair in the corner of my eye.

I need to know. I have to see this again, to find out if I'm going mad or if my husband has just killed two young boys in cold blood. I can't do it any more. I can't hold on, pretending everything is alright, knowing I'm either crazy or married to a serial child killer. I don't know how I've held on this long, but I can feel myself at breaking point, cracking at the seams, ready to explode.

I swallow, step forward and lift up the lid of the bin.

Realising I've jammed my eyes shut, not wanting to see, I gradually open them and re-adjust to the light. I peer inside the bin.

There's nothing but black bin bags.

The cap is gone.

TWENTY-SEVEN

MEGAN

I barely slept last night. Something that was meant to give me closure has sent my mind into a tailspin. Was the cap ever there in the first place? Did I imagine it all along? I hope so. I really do.

But I laid awake all night thinking of the different possibilities. I imagined Chris trying to cover his tracks, having dumped the cap in the bin after killing Riley, then going back later to take it out and hide it somewhere else. Somewhere final. What would he have done? He's a practical guy, and he's not daft. He more than likely would have burned it. Destroyed the evidence.

It was a delusion, I tell myself. It's all down to a lack of sleep combined with some form of post-natal depression. Or maybe some deeper psychological problem. Either way, I'll soon have the answers.

I roll over and look at the clock. 7.54am. Evie's still asleep. I watch her on the baby monitor for a few moments, lying in her cot. She's finally been sleeping through the night this past week or so, which is more than I can say for myself.

I can hear Chris in the bathroom on the other side of the landing, and I roll over and close my eyes for a bit.

I must have nodded off, because I wake when Chris comes back into the room, towelling his hair dry as he stands in the doorway in his boxer shorts.

'She still asleep?'

'Mmmm.'

'The shower normally wakes her.'

'Yeah. She must be tired,' I say, glancing back over at the monitor.

Chris closes the bedroom door behind him and throws the towel to the floor. 'We could always make good use of the time,' he says, as he kneels on the bed, leans over and kisses me.

I try not to react — not negatively, anyway — as I don't want to alarm him.

'I need to get up, Chris. I've got to go into town to get a few things.'

'That can wait ten minutes,' he says, kissing my neck and dropping his arm beneath the bedclothes.

Gradually, I relent, and we spend the next twenty minutes exploring each other's bodies in a way we haven't done since long before Evie was born.

When we're done, Chris rolls over and lies back on the bed. I look at him, not knowing what to think or feel. He brings his hand to his face to scratch his nose, and it's then that I notice the plaster on the heel of his hand. We used to joke that Chris used to be the model for flesh-coloured plasters, as they didn't seem to be the same colour as anyone else's flesh, other than his.

'What's that?' I ask him.

'Hmmm? Oh, I cut myself.'

'When?'

'Out in the garden yesterday. Getting rid of that bloody tree stump.'

'Oh right. You didn't say.'

'Didn't think I needed to. It's only a small cut.'

'How did you do it? On the stump itself?'

'I'm not sure. Probably.'

'Did you clean it properly before you put the plaster on?' I ask, my voice catching in my throat as I speak.

'Of course.'

'Where?'

'What do you mean where? I rinsed the blood off in the sink.'

'Which one?'

He sits up and supports himself on one elbow as he looks at me. 'The bathroom one. What's all this about?'

I look at him as if nothing's wrong. 'Nothing. Just checking, that's all. Don't want you getting an infection or anything.' I lean over and kiss him, hoping this will placate him and convince him that my questioning was entirely innocent.

Somehow, though, things don't quite seem right.

TWENTY-EIGHT

MEGAN

It's weird how seemingly insignificant thoughts keep cropping into my mind. It's almost as if my brain is using it as a coping mechanism. Rather than tormenting itself with the blindingly obvious concern that my husband could be a serial killer, it's instead filling itself with seemingly mundane thoughts. Right now, the main thought going through my mind is that it'll be good for Chris to spend some time alone with Evie while I'm out.

For some reason, I feel as though I need to hide my tracks. I didn't tell Chris I was going back to the doctor. He'd only ask why, and there's no way I could tell him. I park my car in the town centre car park and walk to the doctor's surgery. I even take the back roads, just in case someone sees me.

When I'm about halfway there, my phone rings. I take it out of my bag and look at the screen, but it's a mobile number I don't recognise. I swipe to answer the call and put the phone to my ear.

'Hello?'

'Hi Megs. It's me.'

I recognise the voice immediately, just as she expects me to. Her sheer nerve and arrogance means she doesn't even need to introduce herself.

'Hi,' I say, trying to work out why my sister has decided to ring me now, despite the fact we haven't spoken in years. And what's with all the 'Megs' shit? Does she expect us to suddenly be friends again?

'I know you probably don't want to hear from me, but I thought it was about time we put everything behind us,' she says. She's right about one of those statements, that's for sure. I note there's no apology, no acceptance of the fact that it's her fault we haven't spoken in years.

'I'm just on my way into town,' I reply, as if this is some sort of excuse for not wanting to speak to her. But I'm hardly going to follow it up with 'I'll call you back later'.

'Look, James and I were thinking of organising a family meal. For all of us. We need to put this all behind us. We've still never met Evie, and that's not good for anyone.'

I bite my tongue. Why is it that a new baby in the family means people who've not bothered to speak to you in years suddenly want to pal up again? Because I'm such good company as a sentient adult that you don't want to spend time with me unless there's a gurgling, screaming baby in the room as well?

'I'll have to speak to Chris,' I say.

'I'm sure he'll be fine with it.'

I feel the anger rising up inside me. Who's she to tell me what my husband will think? Then again, I don't have a clue what's going through his mind at the moment either.

Deep down, I know it's a shame we don't talk any more. We used to be quite close when we were younger. We fell out all the time, of course, as sisters do. It was usually due to her bone-headed stubbornness, or her complete inability to recognise that what she'd said could be construed as offensive. Mum used to tell me I was overthinking things, worrying about problems that didn't exist. Part of me wonders just how right she was.

But all I want is an apology, or at least some sort of recognition that what she said the last time we spoke was deeply offensive. I don't want her grovelling on her knees. I just need her to recognise the effect her words had, even if she's not sorry about them.

'Lauren, I don't mean to sound rude, but you can't just brush everything under the carpet. You really upset me that day. And Chris. I don't think you realise.'

'Yeah, I think I got the hint,' Lauren says. 'The fact you haven't spoken to me since then made it kind of obvious.'

I sigh. 'It's only one word, Lauren. And you can't even manage that.'

'What good would it do? Would it mean you weren't

offended any more? What's the point of just saying sorry after things? It's not as if it mends anything.'

'No, but we all make mistakes. Saying sorry is recognising that you made a mistake and pledging to try not to do it again.'

'You think I don't realise I made a mistake?' she says. 'I can say sorry if you like, but I don't know what difference it's going to make to what's happened.'

I stay silent. I know that if I speak I'm likely to snap.

'Megs, you know what I'm like. You know it's not been easy for me to make this call. I don't do regrets. But I'm here. I've called you. I've invited you to come to this family meal and to get everyone round a table together for the first time in years because I want to put things behind us. If you think I'm not sorry for what happened, that's fine. But personally I think actions speak louder than words.'

And, just like that, Lauren the Golden Girl pulls it out of the bag again, leaving me to look like I'm the one who has to swallow my pride. She has a magical ability to turn the tables in situations like this.

I sigh. 'Where and when were you thinking?'

'Sunday lunch at the Forester's?'

'This Sunday?' I say, as if we might be busy, knowing damn well we aren't. The Forester's Arms is a large village pub about six or seven miles from here, which was converted into a new-style gastropub a year or two ago. It's neutral ground — somewhere we've not been in a long time.

'Yeah. This Sunday. If you're free,' she says.

'That's two days away. But I think we are. I'll double-check with Chris when I get back. I'll text you.'

'Great. I was thinking maybe we could all pop back to ours after. I don't know if Mum told you, but we've moved.'

'She did. Sounds lovely. Anyway, I'll text you later. I'm about to go into the bank now,' I say, as I round the corner into another residential street.

And, just like that, my sister is back in my life, as if nothing ever happened. An uneasy feeling in my gut tells me it might not be for the best.

TWENTY-NINE

MEGAN

I sit in the waiting room at the doctor's surgery, feeling like a naughty schoolgirl playing truant. A surge of panicked anxiety rises inside me. Why am I here? What am I doing? It's fine, I tell myself. I just need Doctor Ashford to tell me this is all normal, to tell me this sort of psychosis is a perfectly common feature of post-natal depression. If not, fine. Maybe it's something separate. A different condition. But the one thing it can't be is real.

My heart flutters in my chest, and I pick at my fingernails. I've never been a nervous person. Not up until recently, anyway. Every time a door bangs shut or someone coughs, I jump a little in my seat. I know I'm reaching a cliff edge and I need help. How it's taken me this long to reach the end of my tether is anyone's guess. But what other choice did I have?

I jump again as the appointment screen bleeps and my name appears on it. I stand and hurry towards Doctor

Ashford's room, hoping it'll make my name disappear more quickly.

'So how are you, Megan?' he asks as I enter the room and sit down on the chair next to his desk.

'That's a good question,' I say.

'Is this a continuation of our last appointment?'

'Yes. I think so.'

'Okay. What's changed since we last saw you?'

I sigh. I really don't know how to answer that. Nothing. Everything. Both. Somewhere in between. 'I've been having some worrying thoughts,' I say, eventually, not wanting to meet his eye.

Doctor Ashford shuffles in his seat and leans forward slightly. 'What sort of thoughts? Thoughts of wanting to harm yourself?'

I shake my head. 'No. More... delusions, I guess. Imagining things. Not knowing what's real and what isn't. Being tormented by my own thoughts.'

He nods slowly. 'Can you give me any examples of these thoughts?'

I sigh again. This is it. Make or break. The first time I've ever vocalised my thoughts about this to anyone. After this, there's no going back.

'There's been some news stories recently. The two young boys who were killed locally. I can't stop thinking about it. I don't know if it's because I'm a new mum myself or what, but I... I'm starting to convince myself that my husband is involved somehow.'

If Doctor Ashford finds this shocking, he doesn't let

on. Then again, he probably hears all sorts of things every single day.

'Okay. Was there anything in particular which led you to start thinking that?'

Try as I might, I can't force the words out. However I frame them in my mind, they don't make any sense. It sounds ridiculous whichever way I try. I decide to skirt round the baseball cap.

'He was out when both the murders happened. Not in the house. They were both boys that he taught. He's a teacher. And he's been really funny since it happened. Weird. Distant.'

'That might be because he's upset. If he knew the boys and taught them, he's bound to be affected by their deaths. Have you tried talking to him about this?'

I shake my head. 'No. Well, sort of. He talked to me about Riley, the first boy who died. And when we heard about the second boy, Kai... Well, he sort of broke down.'

'That would explain his odd behaviour. It's a lot of trauma to deal with. People deal with things in different ways. How does he usually deal with grief?'

I think about this for a moment. 'He doesn't. When his dad died he just sort of seemed to accept it. He nodded, said something along the lines of "Well that's that, then" and went back to what he was doing. He didn't even cry at the funeral.'

'That might be a coping mechanism. It's surprisingly common.'

'But it was so different to the way he reacted recently,' I say, before stopping myself going any further.

'Everyone has their breaking point,' Doctor Ashford says. Ain't that the truth. 'And his relationship with his father may well have been completely different to the connection he had with his former pupils. How have you been coping?'

'How do you mean?'

'With the news. I'm sure it's had an impact on you, too. I imagine most parents in the area are worried sick.'

'I guess so. But it's not... it's not like that,' I say. 'I'm more worried about my own state of mind, about the thoughts I've been having.'

'I understand. And these thoughts. Are they intrusive?'

'Yes. Very.'

'Getting worse?'

'I think so.'

He nods. 'I'm conflicted here. I'm tempted to prescribe some mild anti-psychotics, but like anything it's possible some of the drug could be passed to your daughter through breastfeeding. It's not been clinically proven either way, but it's a decision you ultimately need to make for yourself.'

'What would the effects be?'

Doctor Ashford raises his eyebrows and takes a deep breath. 'It's impossible to say, but there's a chance that if trace amounts of the drug reached your daughter she might experience some side effects. My inclination would be to try a very low dose of olanzapine. There are some more common side effects with it, but none of them are serious. You might get some joint pain, increased cholesterol in your bloodstream, increased appetite, tiredness. You might also get some water retention.'

'And they're all things that could effect Evie?' I ask.

'Could. Although, having said that, derivatives of this drug are used to treat breastfeeding women who suffer from nausea and vomiting. I'd recommend trying the lowest dosage — two and a half milligrams — and seeing how you get on. Make an appointment to come back in a week and we'll look at both you and your daughter and work out a plan for how to move forward. How does that sound?'

I nod and force a smile. It's something. At the very least, if the medication does help, at least I'll know it's just my mind playing tricks on me. But I can't shake that feeling that I haven't told Doctor Ashford the full story. Either way, very soon I'll know the truth.

THIRTY
CHRIS

The police came round again today. Two plain clothes detectives, this time. A senior officer called McKenna — an inspector of some sort — and a bloke called Brennan. They wanted to know about safeguarding measures at the school, what the kids were taught about speaking to strangers and walking home on their own. They said Kai Bolton was meant to be dropped back home by his dad, but for some reason that didn't happen. The dad's in pieces, apparently, as I imagine he would be.

They wanted to know if I could think of anyone who knew both boys who might be a person of interest. I got agitated and worked up. I couldn't think of anyone, I said. I desperately wanted to help them, I said, but there was nothing I could do. I told them I'd been racking my brains ever since it had happened, trying to make sense of it all, but I couldn't.

It seemed to me as though they're suspecting everyone. I suppose once they've eliminated the people on their watchlist, anyone's fair game. They asked me almost all the same questions as the other officers asked me a few days ago. I don't know if they're doing that to see who changes their story, or to try and find inconsistencies somewhere along the line, but they seemed happy enough with what I had to say. It's a good job, too.

I've spent a lot of time lying awake at night, getting my story straight. I've gone over and over it in my head, like an actor rehearsing his lines. I've memorised what time I said I left the house. I've pointed to the spot on the map where I was fishing. No, I didn't see anyone walking past, I said. That's the only part where my story could fall down, but it's highly unlikely. No-one ever walks past that spot. I told them I was there the whole time. No, I didn't catch much. Just a few tiddlers. I always throw them back. I do it for the solitude and time on my own, I said. That bit wasn't a lie.

They seemed to believe what I told them. I knew they would — it matched perfectly to what I told them a few days earlier. Besides which, they've no reason to suspect otherwise. I just hope it stays that way. If they uncover the truth, that's it. Everything is finished.

They said they'd ask the press to leave us alone and give us time to come to terms with what had happened. We've had phone calls and knocks at the door at all hours, and it's not doing anyone any good. I've been in touch with a couple of other teachers at the school, and they've had similar experiences. It seems every red-top rag wants inside information on the boys and their families.

I didn't expect much to happen, but it stopped almost immediately. For what it's worth, apparently they're pretty good at leaving people alone when the police ask them to. It's probably in their best interests; they're not going to get any juicy information out of the police if they don't do as they're told. Slowly, slowly, catchy monkey.

I asked what they were doing to find the killer, and they couldn't tell me much. I asked about checking for DNA at the scene. That's something they do regardless, apparently, but they couldn't match DNA on the bodies to any known offenders. There must be hundreds of people's DNA around there, I told them. It's a public area.

Things have a habit of hanging over us like looming spectres at the moment. The number of elephants in the room is unreal. Neither of us are particularly looking forward to this family meal tomorrow. It'll be good if we can put water under the bridge, but I'm really not sure it's a great idea if Megan and Lauren end up being friendly again. Besides which, they always end up falling out. Sometimes things are better kept at arm's length.

I'm just about holding things together right now. I'm keeping it all firmly under lock and key. For now, at least. I don't know how long for. At some point, I know I'm going to crack. I know it's all going to come out and there's not going to be a thing I can do about it. We've all got our breaking points, and I'm getting ever closer to mine.

It takes some getting used to, becoming a new person. Having to lie and keep secrets, pretend nothing is wrong. It's not the way I usually do things — the way I used to do things. But I know this is my life now. From now on, my life is all about secrets and lies. And I have to be comfortable with that. It has to be fine. Because otherwise I'm going to be my own worst enemy, my own biggest liability. If I don't say anything, no-one need know. Things can gradually go back to how they were. Especially if I can stop it happening any more, stop it getting worse.

Quit while you're ahead. That's the old saying, isn't it? I reckon that's the truest thing I've heard in years. I wouldn't say I was 'ahead' by any stretch of the imagination, but the sentiment still stands. The next time could be the time it all falls apart. That could be the time someone sees me. The time my story doesn't quite add up because I've fudged a detail or somehow managed to inadvertently contradict myself. I can't take that risk. I just can't.

Right now, my family needs me. If I don't focus on them, I'll lose everything anyway. What else do I have? Self-destructive behaviour isn't going to help anyone, least of all Megan and Evie.

And that's why I know I have to put all this behind me. I have to put a stop to it. Because otherwise there's only one way it's going to end.

I just can't take that risk.

THIRTY-ONE

MEGAN

My anxiety has been lower since I started taking the medication. I feel calmer. The papers have been full of stories and theories about who might have killed Riley and Kai, and we've been besieged by reporters knocking at the door, wanting to find out what the boys were like at school.

I don't know if I'm imagining it, but Chris has seemed brighter in the last day or so. Maybe he's been fine all along and I've only been able to see the negative stuff. If it was some sort of psychosis, that might be a reasonable thing to happen. I just can't believe that the medication would work that quickly. I was under the impression that antipsychotics were like antidepressants, and could take weeks to work effectively. If they're anything like antidepressants, things get a whole lot worse before they get even slightly better, but that just doesn't seem to be the case. I'm definitely calmer, more rational. I feel like the storm has settled.

I'm not even feeling too anxious about the meal today. I've been worrying about it since Lauren phoned two days ago, but now the day has come I'm actually quite relaxed about it. What's the worst that can happen? Lauren turns out to still be a bitch and we go back to not talking again. Nothing improves, nothing gets worse. But on the other hand, she could give me a grovelling apology, promise to always be there for me and we'll have a lovely meal and leave as best friends. Unlikely, I know.

I decide I'm going to put on my best dress and spend a good hour doing my hair and makeup. I'm not usually one to bother getting tarted up or spending ages slapping stuff on my face, but today I want to make a good impression. If Lauren's going to prove she hasn't changed a bit, I'm going to have my beautiful family by my side, my plastered orange face held high as I sashay the fuck out of there and back to my perfect life. At least, that's what she'll think, if she actually bothers to look.

Even Evie appears to be playing the game. She woke at nine-thirty this morning and has been good as gold. I just hope she can keep it up throughout the day, so I don't end up going from successful supermum to some demented old bitch dragging her screaming brat across the pub.

Chris and I made the most of Evie's lie-in this morning. Until recently, we hadn't had sex in months. Not proper sex. That's twice this week now. If this is the new normal, I can handle that.

He remarked on how I seemed to have changed in the last couple of days, too. He asked if it was anything to do with my visit to the doctor, and I told him it probably was. I've hidden my medication away, though. I don't want him knowing I'm on antipsychotics. I don't know why, but I don't. I told him I had a good chat with Doctor Ashford and he taught me some coping mechanisms and exercises which seemed to be helping. He doesn't need to know it's down to the drugs — as long as the end result is the same.

When we park up at the restaurant, I feel a sense of nervous anticipation. It's not a negative feeling — just a sense that, either way, this will be another marker post in the relationship between me and my sister.

We arrive almost fifteen minutes before we were due to meet, but as we enter the Forester's Arms I can see Lauren and James already sitting at a table on the other side of the restaurant. No matter how punctual and early we are, she still has to go one better.

James is the first to get up, as he marches over to Chris and shakes his hand, before greeting me with kisses on both cheeks — continental style. He's what many women would call the perfect catch: tall, dark, handsome, successful. Personally, I'd go for 'slimy little shit', but then again it's all personal preference.

Lauren waits at the table, but when we get there she greets Chris with the same continental-style kisses her husband greeted me with. This pair really couldn't get any more middle-class if they tried.

'Hi Megan,' she says, holding her arms slightly apart as if to invite me to hug her without wanting to look as though she was the one initiating it. *Take the high road,* I tell myself, and I go in for the hug. It's brief and awkward, and I'm not quite sure who pulls out first but it's done. We've made contact.

If I know my sister at all, she'll now consider everything to be hunky-dory. We hugged, so that means everything's fine now. I'd like that to be true, but it's going to take a lot more than a hug and a pub lunch.

'Is Mum looking after Evie?' Lauren asks. I decided not to mention it first — I wanted to see how long it would take her to bring up the subject.

'Yeah. I thought it might be better that way,' I say, not mentioning the fact that I only asked Mum an hour before leaving. We were going to bring Evie with us, but it just didn't feel right. I didn't want her to become a distraction. Besides which, I want to make sure Lauren wants to see us — not Evie. 'Adults only. You know.'

'Absolutely. Taylor and Theo are with James's sister. They'd only get bored here.'

You could always prop an iPad up in front of them, I want to say, but don't. I made Chris promise me from the start that we wouldn't turn into one of those families who wheel out electronic gadgets in restaurants because they're incapable of parenting.

After more stilted chitchat, we look at the menus and decide what we want.

'I think this is one of those places where you have to order at the bar,' James says. 'Shall I go up?'

He asks Chris to join him, and he reluctantly does. Whether that's because he thinks he's helping by leaving me and Lauren together, or whether he wants to be away from the atmosphere, I don't know.

'Nice here,' Lauren says, after a few moments' silence.

'Yeah. Never been. Not since it's been done up.'

'Us neither. Heard good things, though.'

'Mmmm,' I reply, noncommittally.

'Listen. Before the boys get back. I really just want us to be able to get along again. It's silly how things were before. We should be able to get on, especially with the boys and Evie. It's silly that they've never met their cousin.'

'It is,' I say, stopping myself from adding *And who's fault's that?*.

'I know things must have been hard for you when you thought you couldn't have kids. What I said was a bit silly. I can see how you might have been upset by that.'

'Can you?' I ask, genuinely interested. It's not like Lauren to feel any sort of empathy.

'Of course. We've been lucky, James and I, but I know some other people aren't as fortunate.'

Here we go again, I think.

'Listen, Megan. I didn't mean to upset you. Sometimes I just say things without thinking. And then afterwards

I'm so bloody stubborn that I'd rather cut off my nose to spite my face than I would apologise. It doesn't mean I'm not sorry. It just means… I don't know what it means.'

'Well, if it doesn't mean you're *not* sorry…'

Lauren looks at me, and for a moment I'm not sure whether she's going to apologise or call me a bitch for backing her into a corner.

'Then it means I *am* sorry. Which I am.'

'Don't worry about it,' I say. I thought about saying *thank you*, but that would sound patronising. There's no point in spoiling things. It's taken long enough to get her to apologise for the first time in her life as it is.

Before we get much further, Chris and James return to the table, having placed our order.

'James was just saying we're welcome back to their place after lunch. They've got a couple of new board games they reckon we might like.'

'Oh God, yes!' Lauren shrieks, clearly excited. 'There's this one, called *Liar Liar*. Have you seen that TV programme where the celebrities tell a story about themselves and you have to guess whether it's true or not? It's a bit like that, but better. It's such good fun.'

'Sounds good,' I say, trying not to look at my husband.

THIRTY-TWO

MEGAN

Mum was right. Lauren and James's new place is impressive. All the rooms are good sizes, and their garden seems to go on for miles. It's the sort of place I can see them being really happy in. Most people would be. I don't think I'd fancy their mortgage, though. I'll stick with our three-bed semi.

Even though it's only four o'clock in the afternoon, Lauren and I have already had a couple of glasses of wine at the Forester's and Chris and James have had a beer each, so Lauren decides to crack open a bottle.

'Not for me, thanks. Got to drive home,' Chris says, as Lauren offers him a glass.

'Don't worry about that,' Lauren says. 'You can leave the car here and pick it up tomorrow.'

Chris looks at me. 'Honestly, it's fine. I've got stuff to do when we get back anyway. Maybe another time.'

The bottle of red doesn't go far when shared between

the huge glasses Lauren has given to me, James and herself, so she quickly opens a second and leaves it to breathe.

'This game's so good,' she says, as she takes a box out of the dining room sideboard and puts it on the table. 'Some friends showed it to us at one of their parties. It's amazing the things you find out about people. Even people you thought you knew really well.'

'It's all stuff people never talk about,' James says. 'Things that just don't come up in conversation. It's really cleverly designed, actually.'

The board is small — more of a score recorder than anything else — and the rest of the game seems to consist of cards and pieces of paper.

'Okay, so there's three rounds,' Lauren says, trying to explain the rules. 'In round one, we each have a set of questions and a set of truth or lie cards. We take it in turns to read out the question that's on our cards. Each of the other players has to answer it either truthfully or just make something up, according to whether they've picked up a truth or lie card. The person reading the question has to guess whether you're telling the truth or not. So it could be something like your first pet's name, or the age you had your first kiss. Or the name of your first boss at work.'

James picks up a card. 'So if I pick up my question card. It says "Who was your first celebrity crush, and why?". Then you all pick up a truth or lie card without showing anyone, and you have to either answer truthfully or make something up, depending on whether you pick up a truth or lie card.'

Lauren starts giggling and looks at me. 'Megan and I'll know whether that one's true or a lie, though.'

Then, almost in unison, we both say 'David Soul!' and descend into fits of laughter.

'David Soul?' James asks, not quite getting the joke. I decide it's best I explain.

'When we were younger, Dad used to watch all his Starsky and Hutch tapes back to back. He loved them. We all had to watch them with him, pretending we were enjoying them. After a little while Lauren and I both admitted to each other we only put up with it because we quite fancied David Soul as Hutch.'

'God, I must have only been about nine,' Lauren says.

'Maybe not that question, then,' James says. 'But you get the idea. The second round is similar, but we all write our answers down and the person reading the question has to match up the answers with the players. You'll work it out as we go along. The third round is where things get really interesting. You'll see what I mean when we get there.'

We play the game, laughing and giggling as we go, especially when James admitted that his greatest extravagance was using his student loan to pay for a cleaner to pop in twice a week for three years while he was at university because he couldn't stand cleaning his student digs. I even managed to amaze myself at some of the things I was able to slip past my own sister and husband, both of whom believed me when I said I once dyed my hair bright pink for a breast cancer charity. 'I think I remember that!' Lauren said, proving once again how much notice she takes of other people.

As the game continues, I begin to feel even more at ease. It's made me think that although Lauren might be selfish, shallow and stuck-up, she never means any deliberate harm. A large part of me does feel bad for having been so unwilling to bury the hatchet in the past, but the main thing is we seem to be over that now.

'Okay, round three,' Lauren says, as she shuffles the cards and deals them out. 'This time all the answers are spoken, and the person who reads the question judges which is the best or most shocking answer. You're first, Megs.'

I pick up the question card in front of me and read what's on it. My heart skips a beat and my breath catches in my throat.

What is your biggest secret?

I take two large mouthfuls of wine and read the question.

'Oooh, that's a good one!' Lauren says. 'I can't wait to hear these.'

'You've got to give us yours too,' James says, 'So don't get too scandal hungry.'

'Just for that, I'll go first,' she says, leaning forward and tapping James on the nose. She takes a swig of wine. 'Right. I used to have a boyfriend called Joel when I was about twenty-one. You remember him, Megs.' I nod, even though it wasn't a question. 'Anyway, that summer Mum and Dad took us all away on holiday. Joel came too. One night we were at the pool bar after a night out and we got chatting to these two guys from Newcastle. After a bit Joel went up to bed because he wasn't feeling well. Anyway, long story short, I end up getting back to the room about two and a half hours later. Via theirs.'

I shriek with shock and laughter. 'You had a threesome with them?'

'Yep.'

'Under Joel's nose?'

'Hey, he was on the other side of the apartment block!' she says, laughing.

James looks like he doesn't know whether to be surprised, worried or turned on.

'Jesus Christ!' I say. 'Sometimes there are things you don't want to know about your own sister. Someone pass the brain bleach.'

'Whatever happened to Joel?' Lauren asks, although she should be the one to know.

'He's probably still there, sleeping off his hangover!' I say, laughing. I was so surprised and engrossed by Lauren's story, I've almost forgotten what was written on the card. But looking at it again brings all those feelings flooding back.

'You okay, Megs?' Lauren asks.

'Yeah, fine. Sorry.'

'Come on then, Chris,' she says, nudging him playfully. 'What's your biggest secret?'

Chris looks at me. It feels like our eyes are locked together for an eternity, but I doubt if it's even a second or two.

'I haven't got one.'

'Everyone's got secrets,' James says. 'Just look at Lauren.'

Lauren laughs, although James doesn't seem quite as impressed. 'Tell us,' she says. 'We're all *dying* to hear it.'

Chris takes a deep breath. 'I… once stole some penny sweets from a local shop. When I was about six.'

Lauren and James are almost doubled over, but I'm not laughing. I know that's a lie as much as Chris does.

'That's not your biggest secret!' Lauren says. 'Even the Pope's got bigger secrets than that!'

'Certainly has, if you believe the newspapers,' James murmurs.

'I mean your actual biggest secret,' Lauren says, leaning forward. 'The one you don't want anyone to know. It won't leave this room.'

'I think I'm getting a migraine actually,' he says. 'I wouldn't mind going, especially as I've still got to drive.'

'Oh come on,' Lauren says. 'You don't get to pussy out that easily. Come on. Your biggest secret. The deep, dark secret you've never told anybody. Shoot.'

Chris's jaw starts to tighten and he swallows hard. 'I'm really not feeling great, Megan. Let's just go. It's a daft game.'

I look at my husband. And, for the first time in my life, I'm absolutely certain he's hiding something from me.

THIRTY-THREE

CHRIS

'I hope they didn't think I was being rude,' I say as we pull away from Lauren and James's house and back down their street. 'I just don't feel well.'

I'm trying to keep myself calm and hold back from exploding, but it's growing increasingly difficult. I can't risk it. I still don't know if Megan's forgiven me for reacting physically the other week, and I can't push my luck.

All that talk of secrets and lies was too much for me to bear. I know it was only meant to be a playful game, but sometimes things tend to hit a little too close to the bone at the wrong time.

'Don't worry about it. I'll call Lauren tomorrow and apologise.'

I try to push my anger back down again. I don't need my wife to apologise for me. How fucking degrading can she get?

'Thanks,' I say.

I've never known anything as awkward as today. It turns out the whole thing was Lauren's idea. James told me when we were up at the bar ordering the meals that she thought it would be a good idea to meet up again and put everything behind them. I pretended to agree, but really I just felt sorry for the bloke's stupidity.

He asked how Megan and I were getting on. 'It must be difficult trying to make time for each other with a baby around,' he said, before recounting how for a while he felt as though his own kids had got in the way of his marriage. 'Change everything, don't they?' he said. If only he knew.

I told him everything was fine. I really didn't need any help from the James Mason School of Marriage Counselling. James with his perfect fucking family life and his five-bedroom house with half an acre of land. What he doesn't know is that all that *stuff* doesn't even begin to paper over the blindingly obvious cracks in his own marriage. Cracks? More like gaping bloody holes.

He barely looked at his wife all day. She hardly spoke to him, other than teasing him after she'd had a few glasses of wine and wanted to make him look like a dick. If he thinks that's putting out an impression of the perfect marriage, he's got a lot to learn.

It always amazes me how people think material objects can be a viable replacement for what's really missing in their life. I feel sorry for people like that. If a comfier car or a more prestigious postcode means more to them than what's really important in life, they must have some skewed priorities. Or maybe it's a case of true happiness not being something they're ever able to attain, whereas a new two-grand handbag or round-the-world cruise is easily bought.

It's a shame. I never used to get angry. Not about things like that. But in recent months I've found myself getting increasingly short-tempered with people, objects and situations. A psychologist would probably put it down to a guilty conscience — and they might be right — but it still worries me. Every time I react to something there's a voice inside my head asking me what the hell I'm doing. Not immediately, though. Shortly after. At the time, all I see is the red mist descending, the blood pounding in my eardrums, tunnel vision closing in. I feel the rage bubbling up inside my chest, until there's very little I can do about it.

Sometimes I think about taking myself away from it all. I wonder what it would be like to up sticks and disappear. I'm sure everyone finds the idea romantic on some level, but every now and again I find it hard to resist. I couldn't do that to Evie, though. It wouldn't be fair.

People always say you should live your own life. Don't get trapped in bad marriages or let yourself be unhappy — it's not fair on the kids. If you're weak enough that you can't get through the day without hiding the cracks in your armour, I agree. But surely it's better to have the best of both worlds if you can. Pretend everything's fine. Keep those feelings hidden. After all, when you have kids you stop living for you. You can't afford to be selfish anymore.

The tension makes the back of my head tight. It feels like a cross between a dull headache and someone putting the back of my head in a vice and tightening it ever so slowly.

'I might just go to bed when we get in. Hopefully I'll feel better in the morning,' I say.

'Are you still planning on going in to set up your classroom?'

'Yeah. I'd better. Only got one week left, and there's loads to do.'

Megan nods. 'Need any help?'

'Nah, I'll be alright. Thanks anyway.'

'Might be quicker with two,' she says.

'Honestly, it won't. I know where everything needs to go. It'll be quicker if I do it myself.'

I look over at her and smile, as if to say *That wasn't meant as a dig*. I really need to watch my temper and my tone of voice if I'm going to keep a lid on all this. Because one wrong word or mis-timed comment could bring the whole thing crashing down.

And that's why I'm putting it all behind me. That's why there will be no more. Because the further back in the past it is, the less likely it is to come out. Every day that passes will be another day further from the truth. That's why I can't wait to get home and go to bed. That's why I want another night to pass without notice, for the sun to rise on another day. Another day further from the truth that I cannot risk getting out.

THIRTY-FOUR

MEGAN

It's two-thirty in the morning and I've not even closed my eyes yet. I can't. Chris fell asleep as soon as his head hit the pillow. In a strange way, that made it worse.

If he'd laid awake for an hour or so, or had shown some sort of sign that he was struggling with his conscience, that would be something. We could talk. I could get him to open up. But he came upstairs, took off his clothes, got into bed and went to sleep. Just like that. As if nothing was the matter. As if that look I saw in his eyes when Lauren asked him about his darkest secret wasn't even there.

But there was no mistaking it. You don't know someone for almost your entire life and not spot something like that. It wasn't even subtle. It was a huge flashing beacon to me. Others might not have noticed it if they didn't know him well enough, but I certainly did. It was as if he changed into a completely different person the second the question was asked. He seemed to feel the need to get out of there as quickly as possible and avoid the subject completely.

And that's when I knew. That's when I knew for certain that Chris killed those two boys. I could almost see the memories playing out in his eyes, a glassy reflection of those warm afternoons down by the stream when the lives of Riley Markham and Kai Bolton came to sudden and devastating ends.

The worst thing is, I don't think I saw regret. I don't think I saw sorrow or remorse. What I saw looked more like someone who was worried at being found out. That's what they say about psychopaths, isn't it? Or is it sociopaths? I won't pretend to know the difference. Is that how Chris has managed to pull the wool over my eyes for so long, how he's managed to live a lie and hide this dark secret from me?

They're meant to make good actors, psychopaths. They can switch their emotions on and off whenever they like. In fact, I think I remember reading somewhere that a true psychopath doesn't actually feel emotions. They just watch other people and gradually learn which emotions they're meant to feel at which times. Then they put it on, like a mask designed to show other people they're normal.

At least that would explain things, I guess. It would explain why, when I've known Chris since we were at school, I had no idea he could ever be capable of anything like this. He'd never say boo to a goose. He didn't even engage in disagreements or arguments for the first few years we were together. He'd just shut down and agree with me or keep quiet completely. Now I wonder if those were the years in which he was learning how he was meant to react, finding out what he was supposed to do to look like a normal person. A normal person with feelings and emotions.

I think back over the years to situations and occasions I'd completely forgotten about. Conversations we've had. Places we've been. Those odd times where Chris's behaviour seemed perhaps a little odd, but not for Chris. He was just a shy sort of person who didn't do small talk. It's no biggie; lots of people don't like busy parties or having to force conversations with people they don't know. It doesn't make them a psychopath. Besides which, if he was the perfect actor, why wasn't he able to falsify that confidence?

His dad's death pops into my mind again. The complete lack of any emotion. The stoic, blank face at the funeral. It would have been easy to have copied others' emotions. Everyone was crying. To me, he stood out like a sore thumb as the only one of the near family to be holding it together. It was as if he wasn't feeling anything at all.

Is that why he was able to kill Riley Markham and Kai Bolton? Because he was incapable of feeling any sort of guilt or remorse? How else would someone be able to murder two perfectly innocent children?

That means my theory about his motive is wrong, though. If he's a psychopath he couldn't possibly be driven by his devastation at not having a son, could he? That would involve a deep level of emotion. I'm not a psychiatrist, but somehow the two don't quite sit right with me.

Maybe he's not a psychopath. Perhaps it's something different. Either way, I have to address this uncomfortable truth. I do not know my husband. My husband is a different man to who I thought he was. My husband is a child killer.

I sit up in bed and look over at him. He sleeps peacefully, his mouth hanging slightly open, his shallow breath making the duvet rise a little before dropping again. Is this what a killer looks like? What are they supposed to look like?

A husband should be able to tell his wife anything. We've always tried to talk openly, even if that's been almost impossible with Chris. But do I really want to know the truth? I have to. The truth needs to be told, even if only for Riley and Kai's parents and families. What they're going through must be unbearable.

But I need to be careful. If he's capable of that, he's capable of anything. Right now, I'm at risk and so is Evie.

I look at the baby monitor and see her sleeping soundly in her cot. I get out of bed, grab my glass of water as if I'm going to fill it up, and walk downstairs to the kitchen.

When I'm there, I grab my mobile phone from the worktop where it's been charging, and I unlock it. I dial 101, the police non-emergency number.

My thumb hovers over the *Call* button.

I take a deep breath, then tap it.

THIRTY-FIVE

MEGAN

It seems to take an age for the call to connect. I hear nothing for what feels like minutes but can only have been a second or two, and then the phone rings and connects.

I hear a message thanking me for calling 101, telling me they're connecting me to our county's police force and to press the hash key if I require a different force. I'm willing it to move faster, to connect to an actual person.

Finally, a human appears on the end of the line, and I very quickly realise that I don't know what to say.

'Uh, hi,' I whisper. 'I'm calling because I think… I think my husband might be involved with a crime you're investigating.'

'Okay. Is he there with you?'

'He's upstairs. I've got to be quiet.'

'That's fine. Can you tell me which crime you're referring to please?'

I take a deep breath and realise it's now or never. This is the point at which my life changes irrevocably.

'The murders of Riley Markham and Kai Bolton,' I say.

There's a moment of silence at the other end of the phone.

'Is that Operation Crabtree?'

'I think so, yes.' I recognise the name from the news.

There's another moment of silence. I have visions of the call handler raising her hand and summoning over her bosses. It's been the biggest manhunt in the history of the local police force, and this is the call that could finally catch the killer.

'Can I take your name please, madam?'

'Uh, Megan Miller.'

'And your address please?'

I give her our address.

'Is this number the best one to contact you on?'

I tell her it is.

'Okay, so can you tell me what it is that makes you think your husband is involved somehow?'

I do my best to rattle off everything I know, or think I know. I tell her about the bloodstained cap. I tell her about Chris's box of Riley Markham memorabilia. I tell her about his lack of alibi for both murders. I tell her about his changing behaviour, how he snapped and became physical with me, how I found blood in the sink. As I'm saying it, I realise how mad it all sounds.

She asks me for Chris's details, including his name and date of birth. My heart's hammering in my chest as I speak. I feel dreadful doing it, but not half as dreadful as I'd feel knowing that Riley Markham and Kai Bolton's families don't have the answers they so desperately need.

'He's upstairs,' I say. 'Asleep. We've got a daughter as well. She's just a baby.'

She must hear something in my voice. 'Do you think you and your daughter are in any danger?' she asks.

This question catches me off guard. Even though it's something I've thought about before, the police asking me is something completely different.

'I— I don't know. I don't think so. I don't know. Maybe.'

'Okay. We'll pass the information on to the relevant officers, who'll review what you've told me tonight. Is there anything else you can think of which they might need to know? Are there any weapons or dangerous items in the house?'

'Uh, no. I don't think so. No. Apart from the obvious.'

'How do you mean?'

'Kitchen knives. Garden tools. That sort of thing.'

'Would those things worry you?'

'Well, no-one wants a trowel sticking out the back of their head, do they?' I say, trying to lighten the mood and not seem quite so nervous. I sense the police officer doesn't appreciate my efforts.

'Are there any guns or hunting knives?'

'No. He goes fishing. I don't know if any of that stuff counts.'

I look out through the kitchen window onto our

garden. The streetlight from the road behind bathes the back of our garden in a warm orange glow at night. I look at it and wonder what memories this house will hold for me now. Will Evie and I have to move? I don't see any way in which we can stay here. I'll always be the murderer's wife. We'll have to start again. New names, perhaps.

I realise I've completely tuned out from what the police woman has been saying to me. I hear her saying 'Mrs Miller?', but I can't answer her. I'm frozen on the spot.

In the reflection of the kitchen window, I see my husband standing behind me.

THIRTY-SIX

MEGAN

'What are you doing? Who's that?' he asks, looking at the phone, which I'm holding next to my head.

I end the call and quickly erase it from my call history list.

'I came down to get a glass of water and I checked my phone and saw I had a voicemail,' I say, my cracking voice betraying me.

Chris nods. 'Who was it?'

'Oh, just an old one from a few days ago. The doctor's surgery confirming my appointment. You know how it is, sometimes it says you've got a new voicemail but it's just an old one you haven't deleted yet.'

'Taken you a while to get a glass of water, hasn't it?'

'I had a headache so I went to get painkillers as well. Then I checked my phone, saw the voicemail... I've not been down here long.'

'Twelve minutes,' he says, in a flat monotone.

'Oh. I wasn't counting.'

'I was. You woke me when you left the room.'

'Sorry.'

He looks at me for a few moments, almost quizzically.

'What's wrong, Megan?'

'Hmmm? Me? Nothing. Just a headache, like I said.'

'No, I mean what's wrong?' He takes a step forward towards me. I instinctively step backwards, pressing the edge of the kitchen worktop into the small of my back. 'That. That's what I mean,' he says.

'What is?' My voice is shaky and unsteady like my feet.

'You stepping away from me when I walked towards you. What have I done?'

'I... I don't know,' I answer, completely truthfully.

'Are you sure?' he asks, and I realise I don't know what he's actually asking me. Is he challenging me? Does he know that I know, or is that what he's trying to find out? I can't handle these sorts of mind games. I've got more than enough going on inside my head at the moment without having to deal with this.

'What do you want me to say?' I ask, trying to buy myself some time.

'I want you to tell me what's going on. You've been acting weird for days. Is it because of the doctor? Did they give you some medication?'

'It's got nothing to do with it,' I say, deflecting his question.

'Those sorts of tablets quite often have side effects, Megan. You should have told me you were taking them so I could keep an eye out for things.'

What, so you could gaslight me? I want to say. 'I'm not on any medication.'

'Don't lie to me, Megan. I found the tablets.'

I look him in the eyes and see emptiness. Where once stood my husband, now stands an empty shell.

'You went snooping through my stuff? I put them there because it's private, Chris. You don't just go rummaging through—'

'I lied,' he says. My heart stops for a moment. 'I didn't know anything about any medication, but I said it to see how you'd react. So you have been on tablets.'

'Jesus Christ, Chris. What sort of game are you trying to play here?'

'There are no games, Megan,' he says, stepping forward again. I move to the side to give myself some space. 'Now, what's all this about?'

'Don't even think about it,' I say, my confidence building as I look him in the eye. 'Don't you dare try to make out it's me that's got a problem, that it's me who's hiding things. I don't have any secrets, Chris. But I know yours.'

His jaw tightens as he clenches it, around the same time as I tighten my grip on the knife on the kitchen worktop behind my back. I need to hear it. I need to hear him say it. But I know there's a chance things might not go quite to plan.

'What the hell are you talking about?' he says, as if he genuinely has no idea. But I saw the flash in his eyes just a moment ago. I saw the fear. The realisation. The panic.

'You know exactly what I'm talking about. The long days out fishing. The dash to the shower as soon as you get back in. Putting your clothes straight in the washing machine without me seeing them. The anger. The short temper. I know what you've done, Chris.'

He looks at me, our eyes locked for what seems like an age. I can almost see the cogs turning inside his brain as he tries to figure out what I know, desperately fumbling for an escape route which could save him some face. But what if he doesn't find one? What if he decides there's no other option but to preserve his secret?

'Go on, then,' he says, finally. 'Tell me what I've done.'

The look in his eyes is cold and daring. We both know this is it. We both know this is crunch time. Is this where it all ends? My marriage. My family. My life.

'I know what you did to those boys,' I say, my voice a hesitant whisper, my eyes misted with the beginnings of tears.

'What?' Chris says, his face contorting.

'Riley and Kai. I know what you did to them.'

He cocks his head slightly, his face a twisted wreck of disgust and anger.

'You don't know what the hell you're talking about, do you?'

'I found the evidence, Chris. The blood in the sink. The

drawings and notes. The poor boy's cap. What did you do with it? I know you took it out the bin again afterwards. What did you do? Burn it?'

'Megan, you need to stop this right now…'

'I know what you did. I know you killed them.'

I see something welling up inside Chris. I don't know whether it's anger, realisation or what, but it comes out as a sort of reverse snort. He goes to step towards me and I bring the knife round in front of me, pointing the sharp end of the blade at him.

'Don't come any closer. I'm not afraid of you, Chris, but if I have to defend myself I will.'

'Megan, put that knife down and we'll talk about this.'

'No,' I say, moving it an inch or two closer towards him. 'I'm not putting anything down. I want you to step back away from me.'

'Megan, you're ill. The tablets have clearly given you some sort of —'

'Get back!' I yell, jabbing the knife forward and missing Chris's upper arm by millimetres.

'Megan. Put it down.' His voice is calm and measured now, and that's the scariest thing of all.

'No,' I say, my voice cracking.

'Fine.' Before I can even decode his response, his hand flashes up at lightning speed and grabs my arm, wrestling the knife from me as it clatters to the floor. I reach down for it. Before I can get there, Chris picks me up and holds me against the wall.

He looks deep into my eyes, and I into his. I see nothing but murderous rage.

And that's when I hear the knocking on the front door.

THIRTY-SEVEN

CHRIS

From what I can gather, she'd already phoned the police. That must have been who she was on the phone to when I came downstairs. While I was being read my rights, I overheard one of the officers speaking to her, telling her the woman she'd been speaking to had detected some panic in Megan's voice. When they heard my voice in the room and Megan suddenly ending the call, they made the decision to put the call out to nearby units. The two police officers had been just a couple of minutes from our house.

I told them it was ridiculous. I mentioned the fact Megan has been on antipsychotic medication, but they were having none of it. They wanted to speak to me under caution, they said.

They offered me a solicitor. I turned the offer down. I've got nothing to hide from them and I certainly don't need some smart-arsed Legal Aid shark inadvertently fitting me up. It's all so preposterous, I'm pretty sure I don't have anything to worry about.

I keep seeing that look in her eyes as she told me I'd killed Riley and Kai. She honestly, truly believed it. She actually thinks I killed them.

That was the moment I knew my marriage was over. I'd suspected for a while, but that was the point at which I knew there was no going back. How on earth do you go back from something like that? At that point, all trust is broken. One partner having a secret from the other is bad enough, but when the other suspects a secret and gets it so badly, horribly wrong, there really is no way to repair that damage.

The interview room feels like a claustrophobic classroom without the decoration. The walls are an insipid magnolia, the floor a collection of cheap blue carpet tiles. The ceiling tiles are interspersed with horrendous polycarbonate-covered lighting squares. The whole place looks soulless. I suppose it's hardly surprising.

'You don't seem too shocked or upset, Mr Miller,' the detective asks. It's that same woman who spoke to me before. McKenna.

'About what? Being arrested?'

'About anything much.'

'What do you want me to say? The whole thing's ridiculous. If there was a grain of truth in it I'd have something to worry about, but it's just so laughable I don't really see that there's any point in me getting upset about it.'

'Would it be fair to say that you deny killing Riley Markham and Kai Bolton, then, Mr Miller?' she asks.

'Yes it would.'

McKenna exchanges a glance with her colleague. 'So where were you on the afternoon of the ninth?'

'I went fishing.'

'Anywhere else?'

I swallow. 'No. Nowhere else.'

'Are you sure, Mr Miller? Now would be a good time to tell us.'

I think about this for a moment, then decide the best thing to do is to plead ignorance until they can prove otherwise. I know their game. They make out like they know something, hoping I'll admit to it and tell them everything. In reality, they know fuck all. All they've got to go on is the demented ramblings of my psychotic wife.

'We've spoken to you a couple of times now, Chris, and your story's stayed pretty consistent.'

'That's because I'm telling the truth,' I say.

'Can we just run through it again? For our own benefit.'

I nod. They can try whatever they like. I've got everything straight in my own head and I'm not about to start changing it now.

'Let's start with the day Riley Markham died. You left the house about what time?'

'Just after midday. I had an early lunch then headed out.'

'Who else was home at that time?'

'Megan was.'

'And she was in when you got home?'

'Yes.'

'What time was that?'

'Just after five.'

'That's a long time to spend fishing.'

'I like fishing,' I say. This woman seems to have a knack for winding me up with the tone of her voice. It's a horrible sort of cynicism.

'Where do you fish?'

'About two miles out of the village, upstream. There's a quiet little spot I like to go. A few people fish there early in the morning, but come lunchtime it's deserted. I can sit with the sun on me and enjoy the peace and quiet. I like it.'

'Did anyone else see you?'

'No.'

'What, all day? The whole five hours?'

'It's very quiet up there.'

'Five hours on a warm day in the school holidays and not a single person walked past?'

'Not up that far, no. That's why I go there.'

She settles back in her chair and folds her arms. 'I see. And did you go straight there from home?'

'Yes. I usually walk up when the weather's nice.'

'And you did the same on that day?'

'Yes.'

'Which way do you walk?'

'Down Falconer's Lane to the stream, then up the river

bank.'

'That's a long walk.'

'Like I said. Two miles. It keeps me fit.'

The detective is silent for a moment. Then she looks me in the eye.

'You see, the funny thing is, you were seen speaking to Riley Markham that afternoon, a couple of hundred yards from where his body was found.'

I say nothing.

'Do you want to comment on that?' the detective asks.

'No.'

'Okay. I'll give you a little more information. See if that jogs your memory. You were walking along the side of the stream towards the village at about half past three and Riley was walking the opposite way. You both stopped and spoke to each other for a few seconds, then carried on the way you were going. What did you say?'

I take a deep breath and close my eyes. I decide it's best I tell them the truth. This little part of the truth, at least. 'I said hello. Asked him if he was alright. He said he was heading home. And it was three thirty-three. I remember looking at my watch.'

'Why?'

I don't know why I said that. 'Because he was out on his own. I was going to offer to walk him back home to make sure he got home safe.'

'But you didn't?'

'No.'

'Why not? You were only out fishing. And what were

you doing that far downstream? You didn't come home for almost another two hours.'

'I had to grab something.'

'What?'

'A new reel. I left it in my car.'

'Where was your car?'

'At home.'

'Did anyone see you?'

'I doubt it.'

She leans forward and puts her arms on the desk.

'So you walked all the way home. Two miles. For a new reel. Then you walked back again?'

'Mmmhmmm.'

'Why not just stay at home? You could've gone fishing with the new reel the next day.'

'I was enjoying myself.'

'Enjoying yourself enough to walk eight miles in a day?'

'Yes.'

'Something doesn't quite ring true here. Why didn't you mention this before?'

I run my hands through my hair. 'I dunno. I forgot all about it.'

'You forgot all about walking a four mile round trip, during which you happened to bump into Riley Markham minutes before he was brutally murdered? Forgive me for asking, Chris, but if that somehow managed to slip your mind, it does make me wonder what else you aren't telling us.'

'Do you have any idea what it's like to be told two of your pupils have been killed by a madman? Do you know what that feels like? The guilt I've been carrying around with me, knowing I should have walked him back home? Knowing how selfish it was of me to think my own day was more important and to leave him to... to what happened to him? It looks as though I was the last person to see him alive. That's the sort of thing that eats you up from the inside out.' She looks at me, and in that moment I think I can see that she's buying this. 'Look. I've spoken to your lot three times now. I didn't mention seeing Riley because I felt so guilty about leaving him there, and I knew how bad it would look. But you know it's not me who killed those boys. You know my DNA wasn't at the scenes or on their bodies.'

'We haven't swabbed you for DNA yet, Chris,' she says.

'Well do it then. Go on. Take it now.' I hope this bravado will go my way. What if they took my DNA and did find it on Riley? We stood and chatted for a good ten or fifteen seconds. That's a lot of time for a hair to fall out. Did I touch him? Put a reassuring hand on his shoulder? I don't know. I can't recall.

'We've already placed you at the scene of the crime, Chris.'

'No, you've placed me *near* the scene of the crime. And you have a witness to say that Riley Markham was very much alive at that point.'

'And do you have a witness to say that you didn't go

back afterwards? Unless you can prove you were elsewhere, Chris, it's really not looking very good for you.'

I look down at my hands and realise I've been digging my fingernails into the backs of them. I take a deep breath.

I need to tell them the truth.

THIRTY-EIGHT

MEGAN

I couldn't stay in the house. I just couldn't. All of a sudden it no longer felt like home. I felt vulnerable, scared, alone. The police wanted to take a statement from me to find out what had happened before they got to the house, and I told them I'd rather do it at the station. At that point in time I just wanted to be away from the house.

I didn't tell them about the knife. I didn't see the point. After they knocked, the police called through the letterbox so we knew it was them. Chris went and opened the door, and I put the knife back where it belonged. I told them he'd come into the kitchen, so I had to try and hide the phone. That's why I'd gone quiet. I didn't say that to protect anyone — it's mostly the truth — but I thought it was best to leave out the bit about me brandishing a knife on my own husband.

I told them everything about my suspicions regarding

Chris. I even mentioned the cap, although for some reason I told them I wasn't sure if I'd imagined it or not. Everything is so clouded and hazy in my mind, I don't know what I've been imagining and what's real. It's all a huge mixture of confusion, as if my brain can't handle the sheer magnitude of recent events. They seemed very understanding, but then again I suppose they have to, don't they?

Once they'd finished taking my statement, they ushered us through to another room, which had some children's play things in it. Most of it was designed for slightly older kids, but Evie had great fun putting half the toys in her mouth and throwing the others across the room. A young female officer accompanied us, and took a real shine to Evie. All I could think of was the fact that we'd dragged her out of bed in the middle of the night and that she had already missed two naps. Finally, though, she nods off and I put her down on a folded blanket in the corner of the room.

The young officer — Georgia, her name is — and I have a good chat. She tells me all about her nieces and nephews — she's the youngest of four, and her elder siblings all have children — and we share funny stories about what kids and babies do. It's mostly me just nodding and smiling and giving her looks that say *I know exactly what you're talking about,* and it's at that point that I realise I've been a far more distant mother than I'd ever intended. If anything good is going to come out of this, maybe it's that I will have realised what's important in life.

After a while, Georgia looks at me.

'I hope you don't mind me saying, Megan, but you're taking this very well. I don't know what I would do if I was in your situation.'

'I don't have much choice,' I say. 'Plus I suppose it's something I've kind of come to terms with already. If I'm truthful, I think I've had my suspicions for a while.'

She smiles. 'Anyway. Best to steer onto other topics of conversation.'

She's got a good point. I've already given my official statement, so off-the-record discussions are probably less than ideal.

We spend most of the day in that room. Until I know what's happening with Chris, I can't go anywhere. It's not that I'm not allowed, because I am, but I just feel so in limbo.

It's eight o'clock in the evening before the door opens and the older female detective walks in.

'How are you getting on?' she asks.

'Bored shitless, but feeling safer at least,' I tell her.

She smiles through one corner of her mouth. 'We've spoken to your husband at great length. We've gone over all the detail and compared everything with intelligence we have from elsewhere, and the decision has been made not to charge him.'

In a split second, my entire world falls apart.

'What do you mean not charge him?'

'We've decided not to charge Chris with the murders of Riley Markham and Kai Bolton. He's free to leave.'

'But… I don't understand. Why?'

'Evidence has come to light which shows your husband was elsewhere at the times of the murders. There's no evidence that leads us to believe he was involved.'

'What? I don't get it.' My head is spinning at a million miles an hour. 'He was meant to be fishing. But there wasn't anyone else there. What evidence is there?'

'I'm afraid you'll have to speak to your husband about that, Mrs Miller. I'm not at liberty to divulge the content of statements made during an active homicide investigation.'

I sit back down, before I fall over. 'Where is he?'

'Collecting his things from the custody sergeant. There's a bit of paperwork to do, but after that he'll be free to leave.'

'What, to go home?'

She looks at Georgia, then back at me. 'No, he asked if he could call his mum and step-dad to pick him up. I think he's going back to theirs.'

'And where do I go?'

'That's entirely up to you. Home, I presume.'

I need time to digest this. I need time to take it all in. Surely there's been some sort of mistake. How can he be completely innocent? What evidence is there that he was elsewhere? None of it makes any sense. And now he's not even coming home. He's going to his mum and step-dad's house — something he would never do. He can't stand George, and he's never forgiven his mum for getting together with him so soon after his dad died.

'So what now?' I ask.

'I'm afraid there's not really a lot we can do,' she says. 'As far as we're concerned, your husband has committed no crime. Between you and me, though, I think it would be a good idea for the both of you to sit down and have a talk.'

I thank her, gather our things together and let Georgia lead us towards the exit.

THIRTY-NINE

MEGAN

Chris has stayed away from home plenty of times in the past. There've been school trips, stag dos, all sorts of things. But the house has never felt as empty as it did last night. It wasn't just my husband that was missing; it was my marriage, my family, my hopes and dreams.

Everything we've worked so hard for has been irrevocably ruined. Will I ever be able to look Chris in the eye again? He'll never be able to forgive me, and I'll never be able to fully trust him. Sometimes the police make mistakes. This could be a huge one. What if he did kill Riley and Kai? What if he's going to kill again?

Whatever happened, whatever happens now, I have to come to terms with the fact that our marriage is over. Whether he actually did it or not is almost irrelevant in that sense. How many wives get to call the police and report their husband as a child murderer and expect their marriage to carry on as normal afterwards?

Word of Chris's arrest has already got round the village, too. Regardless of whether he's released, charged or proclaimed innocent by the bloody Pope, some people will always assume he's guilty. He'll never work again. Not as a primary school teacher, anyway, that's for sure. Somehow, it's managed to stay out of the papers. I don't know how long that'll last for, but at least the backlash should only be local, if it happens at all. The British press have a dreadful reputation for splashing huge articles about suspected killers being arrested, only for them to be subsequently proved innocent and released, with their lives left in tatters thanks to the gutter press's appetite for salacious gossip. It wouldn't be fair for Chris to go through that, and I hope it doesn't happen.

Around nine-thirty, the doorbell rings. I look out of an upstairs window, to see if I recognise a car. I don't want to open the door to anyone I don't know. The car parked on the driveway is vaguely familiar. It's not one I've seen many times before, but it's distinctive, and I know immediately whose it is.

I go downstairs and open the front door, and James steps inside. My sister's husband always looks so happy, so confident, but right now he looks downtrodden.

'Sorry. Didn't want to hang around out there in case there were photographers,' he says.

'That's alright. What's up?'

He shuffles his feet. 'I heard about Chris. Thought we should have a cuppa.'

I nod and take him through to the kitchen. It's been

years since either Lauren or James have been round to our house. I'm surprised he even remembered the address.

I make the tea and we sit down at the kitchen table.

'Who told you?' I ask him. 'About Chris, I mean.'

He takes a deep breath, then exhales just as deeply. 'We had the police turn up on our doorstep yesterday afternoon.'

'At yours?'

'Yeah.'

'Why?'

'Well, when I answered the door all they'd say is "it's to do with an investigation". Turns out they wanted to speak to Lauren.'

I close my eyes and try to make sense of this. 'Why on earth would they want to speak to Lauren?'

'That's what I thought. But they wouldn't speak to her in front of me without her permission. She said she wanted to speak to them on her own first. So I went outside. When they were gone, I came back in and she'd clearly been crying. Her make-up was all over the place and she looked haunted.'

James stops speaking, and I give him a few seconds to get himself straight. He doesn't talk, though, and I have to probe him further.

'What was it? What did they want?'

'That's what I asked her. At first I thought something had happened to someone, but she told me it wasn't that. It took her ages to even start to tell me. But then she told me everything,' he says, exhaling heavily. I think I can see tears in his eyes.

'About what?' I ask.

'They told her they'd arrested Chris and were looking at charging him with those little boys' murders. Then they said Chris had given them an alibi, which they needed to verify.'

'What alibi?'

'He told them he'd been with Lauren both times.'

I shake my head and dig my fingernails into the back of my hands. 'Sorry. I don't get it. What do you mean he'd been with Lauren?'

James looks up at the ceiling, clearly trying to hold back the tears. He says the same sentence again, but slower this time. 'He'd been with Lauren both times. They were together. Both times. Having sex.'

I feel an explosion in the pit of my stomach. 'He said that?'

'Yes.'

'But Lauren told them that was a lie, surely?' I ask, knowing exactly what James is going to say next but hoping against hope that he doesn't.

He shakes his head. 'No. She told them the truth. He was telling the truth.'

All of a sudden, I feel as if all life has been knocked from me. I struggle to catch my breath, and my legs feel so wobbly I think I'm going to fall off my chair.

'She told me the whole story, Megan. And he needs to

tell you, too. It's not fair that it comes from me. You need to hear it from him. For your own sake.'

I look at James. He looks just as broken as I do. And in that moment, I wonder how much worse things can possibly get.

FORTY

MEGAN

Not long after James left, I texted Chris.

Come home now. We need to talk.

All credit to him, he did. He must have known by now that I would know. The police will have been to see Lauren, and Lauren would have had to tell James. And one of them would have told me. He wouldn't have been released without Lauren telling the police everything and backing up his alibi. He would have known that his secret would be out, but at least it meant he wouldn't be charged with the murders of Riley Markham and Kai Bolton.

I arranged for Mum to come and pick Evie up between James leaving and Chris arriving. I didn't tell her why — just that I needed time to myself after everything that had happened in the past few days. Thankfully, she didn't argue with that.

When I finally hear his key in the lock, my heart

begins to hammer in my chest. Weirdly, my first thought is that I'll have to get the locks changed. I have no idea how I'd do that or what it would cost, but there's no way I can have Chris letting himself back in whenever he feels like it.

I hear him kicking off his shoes and walking through to the kitchen, where I'm waiting, sitting at the kitchen table with two cups of tea.

'Milk, two sugars,' I say to him. He nods and sits down.

We sit in silence for almost a minute before I speak.

'Come on, Chris. You're not stupid. You know what this is all about. Man up and tell me yourself.'

He looks like a broken man, but I can't say I'm sympathetic. This is all his doing. All of it. It's his secrets and lies that have caused this.

He takes a deep breath, and speaks as he stares into his mug.

'On the day Riley died, I did go fishing. I was only there for a couple of hours, though, and then I headed back towards the village. We'd arranged that Lauren would pick me up from the car park at half three.'

'Why?' I ask.

'Why do you think,' he replies, more as a statement than a question. 'On my way to the car, I saw Riley. He was walking past the stream towards his house. I was going to ask him if he wanted me to make sure he got back safely, but I was already a few minutes late. So I didn't. Jesus Christ, I've replayed that moment in my head a million times over. Why didn't I just walk him home? It was a couple of minutes away, if that. Lauren could have waited. But all I could think about was getting my fucking leg over. And because of that, he died. That's why I wanted to see his parents. I felt guilty. Worse than guilty. I felt responsible. But I couldn't do it. I just sat in the car outside their house, looking at their front door. I couldn't do it. I couldn't go in. I was so fucking weak I couldn't even bring myself to do that.'

There are tears rolling down Chris's face as he speaks, but I don't feel even an ounce of sympathy for the man who was once my husband.

'Was that the only time?' I ask him, knowing damn well what the answer is going to be.

He shakes his head. 'No. I was with her when Kai died, too.'

'Did you see him?'

'No, I hadn't seen him since school finished.'

I nod. Now that Chris is beginning to open up, I can finally see what's the truth and what's a lie.

'How many times?'

He runs his hand through his hair. 'I don't know. I honestly don't know. It got to the point where it was three or four times a week. James was working away, you were... Well, we haven't been as close since Evie was born.'

'That's your excuse?'

'No. It's my reason. There's a difference.'

'Where did you go?'

He sighs. 'All sorts of places. Never at either of the houses though,' he says, looking at me, as if this makes it all fine. 'There's an old industrial unit just off the bypass. Used to be an auction storage warehouse, but it's been closed a couple of years. There's nothing else around there, but it's got a few parking bays. She used to park up, and we… Well. You know.'

'No, I don't know. You're going to need to tell me.'

He swallows. 'We had sex.'

'Three or four times a week?'

He nods.

'When you told me you were going fishing?'

'I was going fishing. We just sort of tied the two in together.'

'Oh how romantic,' I say, starting to find my confidence. 'Tell me. How the hell did it even start? We haven't spoken to Lauren in years.'

'She texted me one day. She got my number from your mum, apparently. She said she wanted to put everything behind her and bring the family back together again. We met up. I went round to the house one day after school and said I'd tried to put out some feelers, but you weren't having any of it. Every time her name came up your face looked like you'd been poisoned.'

'You went round after school?'

'I told you I had a couple of late meetings. I didn't technically lie. But nothing happened. Never in the house. And anyway, James was there. And your mum.'

'Mum was there?' I say, my breath catching in my throat. Was she in on it as well?

'Yeah. She's always wanted you two to get back together. She doesn't know about any of this, by the way. Jesus Christ, she'd castrate me if she found out. We had a chat about it, and I said it was probably best to leave it for now because Evie was still young and we had lots going on. I didn't want you getting upset. But me and Lauren carried on seeing each other.'

'*Seeing* each other,' I say, with a heavy emphasis on the first word.

'Yeah. Well, you know.'

'You mean fucking each other.'

He doesn't respond to this. 'After a while she said she was going to get in contact with you directly. She thought maybe if she actually picked up the phone herself and sounded remorseful, you might be more willing to do something about it. And it worked. For a bit.'

'That day at the restaurant,' I say. 'By then it had already been going on… how long?'

'Three months.'

I stare open-mouthed at Chris. 'Yet you both managed to sit there and not say a word? Jesus Christ, you even went up to the bar with James and left me sitting with Lauren. She was laughing and joking, and all along she knew she'd been screwing my husband for *three months*?'

'It wasn't like that. What choice did we have? Sit you both down and tell you?'

'Don't tell me you thought you were going to get away with this forever,' I say.

'No, of course not. I'd already put a stop to it by then. I told her we couldn't do it any more. Did you not notice how she barely said a word to me all day, and when she did it was almost teasing?'

The realisation hits me like a breeze block to the face. 'The game. She drew that question for me about your biggest, darkest secret and you wanted to go home.'

'Yeah. By then she'd had a few glasses of wine and it was getting daft. She tried coming on to me in the kitchen, and then she tried pulling that little stunt. I don't know whether she switched the cards or what, but I wasn't impressed.'

We sit in silence for a minute or two as I try to digest what Chris is telling me. Both my husband and my sister have betrayed me. I've lost everything. But still, my brain resorts to trying to think through things logically. Maybe it's a coping mechanism.

'Hang on a second,' I say, looking at him. 'Why would the police believe any of this? Surely they're not just going to accept an alibi from your own sister-in-law. What's to say you hadn't paid her off or forced her to give you an alibi?'

I know this isn't the case, and I can tell Chris is telling me the truth about his relationship with Lauren, but the police's actions don't make any sense.

He closes his eyes and rocks his head. 'Fuck's sake, Megan, why do you have to ask questions like that?'

'Because I want to know the answer,' I say, knowing damn well I really don't.

He takes a deep breath. 'There were pictures. Lauren has this thing where she liked to take pictures of us having sex. I don't know why. She just did.'

'And she showed these pictures to the police?'

Chris nods.

'Why the hell would you let her do that? Surely you knew she could use it as some sort of blackmail against you in the future?'

'God, I don't know. The first time I was just so turned on I would have let her put a fucking advert in the *Sunday Times*. After that, what was the point in refusing? She had the first lot anyway.'

'Typical man,' I say, totally not regretting my comment. 'Is that it? You've told me everything?'

He sighs. 'Yeah. I've told you everything.'

'Does it feel better?'

'No. Not really.'

'Good,' I say, standing up and throwing the remains of my cold tea into the sink. 'In that case, you can get out of my house.'

Chris looks at me, stands, and heads towards the front door.

FORTY-ONE

MEGAN

When Chris leaves, I head straight for the wine rack. I know alcohol's probably not the answer, but right now there are no answers and alcohol will help blot out everything that's going through my mind.

It sounds weird to say, but I really don't know if Chris looked remorseful or not. Sure, he definitely *tried* to look remorseful, but I don't know if that was just him putting on an act. He's already proven himself to be good at that recently.

More to the point, I don't know how I feel. Crushed. Broken. They're all words I could use, but right now they have no meaning. The world has lost its flavour, been wiped of its colour.

I rummage around in the cutlery drawer for a corkscrew, but I can't find one. I grab handfuls of the cutlery and throw them on the floor until I see the corkscrew hiding at the back. I jab it into the top of the bottle and twist, yanking the cork out and slopping wine over my hand. I lick it off, grab a glass from the cupboard and fill it almost to the top. I down the glass and refill it.

Within seconds my head starts to feel less muddled. I didn't think alcohol took effect this quickly, but it might be different when you down an entire large glass of wine in one hit. I should try it more often.

Now I'm thinking more clearly, I feel more angry. Before I even realise what I'm doing, I pull my shoulder back and punch the kitchen door as hard as I can. It's the only time I've been thankful for our cheap hollow-panelled doors, because my fist goes straight through into the cavity, leaving a nice hole as I pull my fist out, the sharp edges of the wood leaving white scrape marks along the back of my hand.

My head starts to buzz. I see bright lights, images, but none of them clear.

I take a couple of steps back — stagger, in fact — and try to catch my breath. I didn't realise I'd been almost hyperventilating. I try to calm myself as I come to terms with my violent outburst. That's not like me. I don't get violent.

My head buzzes again, and I reach for the glass of wine. My knuckles brush the stem of the glass and I watch it wobble as I grasp for it. I miss, and the glass crashes to the floor, the deep red liquid pooling on the tiles.

The image makes my head buzz again. I watch as the wine changes form slightly. The tiles get smaller. I see water. I smell sun.

And suddenly it all starts coming back to me.

FORTY-TWO

MEGAN

That day, the day that Riley Markham was killed, I'd been out. I remember now. I got home and put the washing machine on. It was on an hour's cycle and bleeped to tell me it was finished just as Chris walked through the door. He got home just after five. I remember that, as it was earlier than I expected. So I must have got home about four o'clock.

Everything's a horrible mixture of images, and I can't make head nor tail of it. I get flashes in my mind, some of them real, some of them made-up. I see Chris coming home. The flashing police sirens. Riley's lifeless body.

All the days seem to roll into one. I know I'd been walking. If I could remember exactly where I'd gone, I could try to make some sense of it all. I often walk down by the stream, but I don't think I did that day. I would have remembered. And, in any case, if Chris had been walking down there to Lauren's car at around half-past three and I got home around four o'clock, he was playing a very risky game. There was a good chance I would've seen them. But I didn't. Did I?

My brain seems to have blanked out all sorts of things, but I would have remembered that. You don't see your husband climbing into a car with your estranged sister when he's meant to be out fishing and not remember it.

But what if my brain's blanked that out too, as some sort of coping mechanism? Was it protecting me from what I already knew? When Chris told me about the affair with Lauren, I was stunned. Of course I was. But I shocked myself at how quickly I managed to compose myself and question him about it. Even now, I'm more numb than anything. I've not shed a tear. Is that normal? Is it just my mind's way of trying to cope with things?

There's lots more that doesn't make sense. Just because Chris had been having an affair with Lauren, that doesn't mean he didn't kill Riley and Kai. They can't pin down the exact minute that Riley was killed — just that it was before his body was found around half-past four, and after Chris saw him at half-past three. How do we know Chris was telling the truth about that? How do we know the witness wasn't mistaken? Chris could have used that to his advantage, as it'd allow him to use the Lauren alibi. Sure, he's ruined his marriage and my family by having to admit to his infidelity, but who wouldn't if it meant they got away with murder? My family was already ruined. And, if I'm honest, so was our marriage.

What if he paid the 'witness' to say that? I still don't

know who the witness was. Maybe it was a friend or associate of his. That'd be the perfect witness, wouldn't it? A friend of his who is seemingly incriminating him with his witness testimony. Why would a friend do that, unless he was telling the truth? There is only one reason: because the real truth is far more sinister.

If the police don't know exactly what time Riley died, what use are the photos in proving anything? Even with time stamps, how do they know categorically that Chris didn't kill Riley before or after being with Lauren? It would take mere seconds to kill a small child.

I'm amazed at how quickly the police seemed to discount Chris in the face of all the evidence. There must be something they're not telling me. Something he's not telling me. But what sort of detail would he leave out? And why? He's already admitted to sleeping with my sister on a regular basis. He admitted they took photos of themselves. He admitted he'd been lying and sneaking around. Why would he leave out more detail? What could be worse than that?

There must have been a terrible mistake. There must have been.

I can feel my anxiety growing again. Nothing makes any sense. None of it. Everything seemed to piece together perfectly in my mind. It made absolute sense that it was Chris, even if I didn't want to believe it. Even if I had to convince myself that was the truth. I *had* to convince myself of it.

Why? *Why?*

Because deep down, if you look hard enough, if you want to see it, you'll always find the truth.

I see it clearly now.

Riley's blood-stained cap in our bin. The blood in the sink. It all pointed to someone in this house being the killer.

And that's why I had to believe it was Chris.

Because otherwise…

FORTY-THREE

THE FIRST TIME

The strong sun on my head beats me into a soporific state. It's like a drug. A drug that I need. It gives me energy, but at the same time it takes me away to another place.

I walk aimlessly. When I'm in this state, I switch off. My mind goes elsewhere. This, though, is how I want to be. This is me at peace. This is where I'm comfortable. This is where I can stop fighting it, stop pretending to cope. Stop trying to live a normal life.

This is the only time all my senses open up. The sun feels stronger. The air smells fresher. The stones on the loose footpath poke and prod at my feet through the soles of my sandals.

I'm alive.

It's a strange feeling, being both so incredibly energetic yet sedate and calm at the same time. I guess this is what being in a trance feels like. A tranquil euphoria.

When I feel like this, nothing registers. I'm here, in the

moment, in the here and now. The previous seconds and minutes do not exist, and the near future will register only fleetingly. It gives me an extraordinary sense of freedom.

One chance.

But there's an underlying current of emotion. It's something I can sense, but not put my finger on. It's negative. That's all I can work out. Perhaps anger. Perhaps sadness. Perhaps hatred. Whatever it is, it's the underlying emotion which compels me to come out here, urges me into this invigorating, calmative state. It's the nucleus of what I am right now, the delicate explosive that's wrapped in sunshine and calmness, lest it ignite and take everything else with it.

We had one chance.

Even trying to explain my thought process makes it both simpler and more complicated at the same time. Sometimes there are things which can't be put into words.

Something flashes across the front of my mind. An image. A snapshot. A faint memory.

I ruined our one chance.

It's like seeing a flash of lightning illuminate a room for a split second. It feels like a thousand volts searing through my body. It smells of anger. It reeks of regret, jealousy and agonising pain. It feels familiar, yet at the same time I don't recognise it. It hurts. It fills me with pain. It makes me want to wail in agony.

I let him down.

Our one chance, and I failed him.

I can no longer feel the sun. The stones on the footpath

turn to cotton wool. The air fills with sulphur and the stench of death.

The death of me.

I cross over the footbridge, feeling myself rise and fall as I do so, hearing my footsteps echo against the water underneath, but feeling no sensation through my feet. I walk a little further along the footpath and I see him in front of me. I vaguely recognise him from around the village. He looks happy. This is how my boy should have looked. Chris's boy.

But I let him down.

I ruined our one chance.

We had one chance.

One chance.

He speaks to me, greets me. I say hello back. Then I watch. I observe. I notice the tiny, seemingly insignificant little things that only a parent could notice. And, for a moment, he's mine. He's the boy I was meant to give Chris. The son we never had. The family I failed.

I want to love him.

He gives me a look as though I'm mentally disturbed and tries to push past me. A switch flips inside me and before I know what's happening I've put my arm around his waist and clamped my other across his mouth.

It's instinctive. Animalistic.

I pull him to the floor behind the bushes and press my forearm to his neck. I can't have him screaming. Not now.

There's no way back.

No way back.

FORTY-FOUR

MEGAN

I find myself sitting in the middle of my kitchen floor in a cold sweat. I feel as though a torrent of memories has hit me all at once. I don't know how to cope. I don't even know what to think or believe anymore.

It's like waking up from a dream, not quite knowing what's real and what isn't. When you wake up from a dream, you have the luxury of gradually realising you're safe, becoming aware that what your mind just played out to you wasn't real. This is the opposite of a dream. This is a nightmare. With every passing second comes the dawning realisation that the memories played out by my mind are far from fantasy.

It feels like watching a movie, seeing an actor playing me, looking on as she pins Riley Markham to the ground, his face turning red, then purple, then blue. Listening as his windpipe whistles and his fingers dig into her arms, desperately trying to get a purchase on the fabric.

Watching through her eyes.

It doesn't play out like any other memory. It's not like thinking back and trying to remember how things looked and felt. It's a passive experience, watching on as the memory plays itself out. I can only see. I can't feel. It has no emotion or feeling attached to it. It just is.

It's so distant, so remote. Yet I know it's me. There's no mistaking it. I know instinctively that this happened. And suddenly it all starts to make sense.

The bloodstained baseball cap in the bin. The blood in the sink. The links to us. To this house. They were links to me.

I remember taking the cap out of our wheeliebin. I remember bagging it up and throwing it into the bin outside the post office.

I let him down.

I was right. I was seeing these things, thinking these thoughts as a coping mechanism. It was my brain's way of making sense of things. But not because there weren't answers. It was because I couldn't acknowledge the answers. I wouldn't let myself see it.

I press my face against the cold tiled floor and let out an animalistic groan. I never meant any of this. I'm not a killer. I couldn't kill a child.

But I did. Twice.

This body did. This physical being did. Not me. Not real me.

I don't know what real me is anymore. My life is

unrecognisable. Everything has collapsed. Everything I knew to be true is gone. And it's all because of me.

I let him down.

I see Riley's face in the reflection of the floor tiles. His blue face looks longingly at me. There's desperation in his glassy eyes. I hear the breath rush from his crushed windpipe, then back in. He looks at me and whispers, his voice pained and hurt.

Mummy.

I watch as the tear drops from my eyelids and splashes onto his porcelain face. He looks like he's underwater, sinking further down, getting further away until I see the last flash of blue from his eyes.

I let him down.

Silently, I'd promised Chris a boy. He'd wanted a son so much.

We had one chance.

I blew our only chance. I let him down.

How could I ever be expected to bond with a daughter when I'd so desperately wanted to provide him with a son? I could see the look in his eyes when the sonographer said those words. I watched the hope build in the weeks and months afterwards, knowing that inside he was desperately praying she'd been wrong. And I saw that face again in the hospital when she was born. At what was meant to be the happiest moment in both our lives, all I could think was that I'd failed him. We'd been given one chance when we thought we had none, and I'd still managed to let him down.

All our friends have boys. I see young boys everywhere. Every time I see a young child out playing in the street or kicking a ball around the park, it's boys I see. It's as if their parents are teasing me, showing me that they've got the one thing we wanted. The one thing he wanted. The one thing I desperately wanted to provide for him.

Everyone else had been blessed. Every other family unit was complete. No others had the huge gaping hole I'd left in ours.

Chris always told me he didn't mind. He told me he'd love our child unconditionally, regardless. But he didn't need to tell me the truth. I could see it. He's a good man. He didn't deserve this. He didn't deserve me.

I let out another cry as I feel an intense rage and anger burning inside me. A rage I can do nothing about. An anger directed only at myself.

I let him down.

It should have been us. It should have been me. He should have been ours. The rage continues to build as I pummel my fists into the tiled floor. The pain inside persists, so I lift up my head and bring it crashing down onto the tiles. Then again. And again.

I keep doing it until the blood runs into my eyes and mouth, its metallic taste choking me as I rest my throbbing head in my own blood and weep.

FORTY-FIVE

THE SECOND TIME

It feels odd calling it that, because I don't really remember the first time. The only way I can describe it is that I have this innate knowledge that it happened. It's more of an acceptance, in the same way that you know one plus one is two, without having to think about it or work it out. It just is.

But it's more than that, because it's not something that I'm always conscious of. It's become a part of me, something that goes on without me even realising it. Like a heartbeat. Or a breath. It carries on without you noticing, but as soon as you notice it, you can't un-notice it without distraction. A breath is more, you see, as you can control it as soon as you notice it. That's not so easy with a heartbeat. I'd go so far as to say impossible. This is more like a heartbeat. Imagine a heartbeat that you can only notice at certain times, under specific conditions. That's the closest

I can get to describing what it's like, and even then I'm still a million miles away.

Although I don't recall the specifics from the first time, I can still feel the emotions. I remember the huge surge of anger tied with grief, and the resentment that united them. I can feel the compulsion that washed over me, the realisation that I had no choice. It was a beautiful sort of acceptance, almost like the poetical embrace of impending death. Imagine a moment from a film, in which a character realises they are dying and comes to accept it peacefully and with tranquillity. It's not something I wanted to accept was happening, but I had no choice.

I went with it.

And now it's like an itch I need to scratch. The release it gave me was huge; one I didn't even know I needed. You don't always realise how bad your back is until the masseuse digs his thumbs in. And then there's no going back — you're fully aware of every single tight muscle and knot.

I feel as though I'm floating across the footpath. No sensation comes from my feet. The sounds begin to dull and my vision starts to drain of all colour. Smells disappear. It's like being cocooned. The only thing that appears in colour is the young boy standing at the edge of the stream, watching with glee as the water rushes over the pebbles.

I continue to float towards him, careful not to make a sound I couldn't hear anyway. I stand right behind him, barely inches away, but he still doesn't know I'm there.

I look at him, standing out here on his own, left to fend for himself by parents who don't appreciate the son they were blessed with.

He should have been ours. We wouldn't have let him walk down here on his own while we sat at home worrying more about ourselves than our young son. They don't deserve him. They don't deserve any of it.

I imagine him sitting at our dining table, telling us about his day at school. We're so proud of him. Our son.

But he isn't our son. I know he's not. He's the unwanted, unloved boy who other parents should have been blessed with. Parents like us.

We could have been so happy. We would have loved him.

Our son.

His parents don't know how lucky they are. They don't know the hurt and humiliation they've caused. They don't deserve him. He doesn't deserve to live.

In one fluid movement, which comes about entirely subjectively, my arm goes around his neck and I lift him up in the air. I pull my forearm towards my chest, constricting his windpipe, crushing as hard as I can.

He gurgles like a drain as he begins to go limp. My arm is agony, and I can't hold on much longer. With my other arm, I reach over and grab a length of damp rope that's been discarded in a bush, and pull it round his neck. I cross the ends and pull tight as he drops to his knees, desperately scrambling to free the rope as he gurgles breathlessly.

I see him turning red, then purple, but not blue. Not yet.

I tie a double knot in the rope at the back of his neck, take a step back, then swing my leg, aiming it at his head.

He falls into the stream silently, as if the lights have just been switched off.

FORTY-SIX

MEGAN

Everything seems perfectly clear yet totally opaque at the same time.

I accept what happened. I know it happened. I don't remember it in the conventional sense, but now everything makes perfect sense. I had to believe it was Chris. My battle was completely internal. I needed to believe Chris killed Riley and Kai, because I had to make sense of the evidence in front of me. The alternative was to acknowledge the truth and destroy myself in the process.

But now I have no choice. The police have released Chris. They know he didn't kill those boys. And there's no-one else my brain can try to convince me was responsible. I've had to accept the truth. I've had to accept it was me.

Regret's a funny word, isn't it? I don't know if I regret what I did. I have no emotional feeling towards it. But I do know it was wrong. And I know what happens next.

It's only a matter of time before the police join the dots and work it out. And then what? Megan Miller, the child murderer. Evie will grow up without a mother. All she'll have is a father who didn't want her in the first place. A father who's more concerned with getting his leg over the sister-in-law than he is being the dutiful family man he portrays himself as. And what chance does Evie have when Chris loses his job? Because that's what's going to happen. There's no way in hell he can carry on working at the school. Not now. He won't be able to get a job elsewhere, either. 'Why did you leave your last position, Mr Miller?' 'Oh, it's quite simple, really. My wife murdered two of the pupils.'

The community has already been torn apart. My family — well, I can put that down to Chris — but this will prove to be the icing on the cake.

I look down at the blood on the kitchen floor, the edges of it beginning to dry on the tiles. My first thought is that it's going to stain horribly, but what does it matter? I won't be here to worry about it. I'll have bigger messes to try and clean up.

I've ruined everything. I've pushed Chris away and into the arms of my sister. I called the police and reported him as a murderer. I've ruined his life. And all because I wanted to make it up to him. I did it for him.

I can't bear to spend the next fifty-odd years rotting in a jail cell, with only sporadic visits from my daughter to look forward to. I don't want her growing up having to go through that. Prison is no place for young girls.

And that's if Chris even allowed her to visit me. He could tell her whatever he wanted. He could tell her I'd died, or gone to live somewhere else and she wouldn't know any different. They could move away, change their names and Evie would never know her true identity. She could even grow up and read articles about what happened and not realise the connection. And where would that leave me? Still sitting in the same jail cell, rotting away, dodging the razor blades in my porridge.

That's not a thought I can countenance. It would be much better for everyone if I wasn't there. Chris could tell Evie — quite truthfully — that I'd died. He could tell her how unwell I'd been, that I'd done my best for both of them but it just wasn't to be. He wouldn't need to tell her the whole ugly truth. That's the only bit that matters. That's the only bit that's truly me.

Some people might call it the coward's way out. They might think I was trying to evade justice, not wanting to answer for my actions. But justice has already been done. My life is ruined. My family is in tatters. No time spent in a concrete room is going to make that any better or worse. Besides which, I can't answer for my actions. I only have the reasoning and justification I gave to myself, and I'm well aware that no-one else will understand that.

Chris wanted a boy — desperately wanted a boy — but got a girl. I let him down. The time he spent away from home after she was born told me that much. He resented me. All I wanted to do was make it up to him, and I failed. It made sense at the time. It made perfect sense.

Whichever way this ends, my marriage is over. My life as I know it is over. There's still a chance the police won't discover the truth. The chances are slim and the net is closing in, but there's still a chance. If I hand myself in, Evie's life will be ruined before it's even begun. Chris's life and career would be torn apart. The local community would be left in tatters.

But I could go. I could end it all by ending my own life. If the police found out the truth after my death, would they announce it? What good would it do? Perhaps they'd try to make things easier on Chris and Evie by keeping that little detail under wraps. There must be ways and means.

My death would, undoubtedly, have a profound effect on Chris and Evie and the rest of my family. But, in time, they'd move on. They'd be able to build a new life whilst sparing everyone else even more hurt.

My medical notes will show a recent history of post-natal depression and the prescription for antipsychotic medication. A huge percentage of mothers with post-natal depression end their own lives. I've seen all the articles, read all the books.

This is the only way it can end. This is the only way out that gives some possibility of hope for everyone else, even if there is no hope left for me.

I know what I mean to do.

This is how it has to be.

FORTY-SEVEN

MEGAN

For the first time in as long as I can remember, I'm thinking clearly. I stand up and walk across to the other side of the kitchen, the dried blood sticking my feet to the floor. I rummage through the stack of bills and unopened letters for a sheet of paper. There aren't any plain sheets, so I make do with a couple of opened envelopes.

I pick up a pen and begin to scribble down my thoughts. I'm not sure they make any sense at all, but right now that doesn't matter. I need to get this out of my head and onto paper, so somebody else can read it. They'll have all the time in the world to try and make sense of it. I don't have that luxury.

The pen moves quickly across the paper. I barely recognise my own handwriting. It's a mish-mash of thoughts and probably mis-spelled words. It doesn't matter. All that matters is that I say what I have to say. It wouldn't be fair on them if I said nothing. They need to know I'm doing it for them, just the same as I did everything else for them. This time, though, it will work. This time, eventually, they will see the benefit. They just won't know it.

I go upstairs to the bathroom cupboard and take out two boxes. Then I open my sock drawer in the bedroom and rummage through it to find the third box. I put them in my pockets, taking out my mobile phone and leaving it on the bed.

I head downstairs and put my shoes on. It seems a bizarre necessity, after trailing bloody footprints around the house. Part of me wants to get the cleaning products out and get rid of the footprints, but I stop myself. Doing anything else would open up the possibility of me changing my mind. Might I even do it again? No. I don't think so. But I can't take that risk. Whatever happens, I have to put a stop to this right here, right now.

I close the front door behind me and walk down the road towards the footpath that leads to the river.

When I get to the edge of the stream, I look to my left. I imagine, a mile or two further down, Chris sitting at the side of the river with his fishing gear, staring off into space as he tries to make sense of everything that's happened.

It hits me that I'll never get to say goodbye to Evie. Not properly. But deep down I know that's probably for the best. If I saw her again I'd only change my mind, and that wouldn't be good for anyone, least of all her. This is the best option in the long-run. As much as it pains me, as much as it tears me apart, this is best for her.

Sooner or later, their memories will become hazy. Life will go on. Chris and Evie will have a new life. They'll find happiness again.

Off to my right-hand-side I can hear children playing in the park. Playing with their parents watching over them, no doubt, wary of the killer that lurks in their midst. Still, life goes on. With a little adaptation and an extra parental eye, this day can be like any other. Things need not change. Their way of life doesn't have to alter.

That thought gives me some internal peace. Sooner or later, their memories will fade too. Their parents will take their eyes off them for a few moments while they chat between themselves. One day, they'll nip over the road to grab ice cream for the kids. They'll only be a couple of minutes. Perhaps later they won't even need to watch over them at all. The perceived danger will be but a distant memory.

They won't know it just yet, but that danger will have passed long ago.

I stand at the edge of the water, watching it ripple over the pebbles and pool in the deeper areas. The undulation of the bed of the stream is almost as mesmerising as the water itself. I empty the first two blister packs into my hand, put a handful of tablets into my mouth and scoop up water from the stream to wash them down with. The olanzapine won't be enough to do the job. Not at the dosage I'm on.

I follow it up with a box of paracetamol and the sleeping tablets. The water from the stream doesn't taste anywhere near as crisp and clear as it looks, and I gag a little as I try to wash down the tablets. Eventually, though, I manage it.

The water drips off the edge of my chin and into the water, making small splashing sounds as it does so.

I take off my shoes and step down into the water, feeling the pebbles beneath my feet as the bed of the stream shifts slightly. I put my hands down and feel the water passing over them. Gradually, I get to my knees before sitting in the water. It's cold, refreshing.

I lie back and let the cool water wash over me.

FORTY-EIGHT

Dear Chris and Evie,

You might find this before they find me. If you do, please don't worry. I'm safe now. Everyone is safe now.

You will be asking yourselves all sorts of questions. You probably will for years. I don't have those answers for you, but I will try to help. If you ever ask yourself if there was anything you could have done to have stopped this happening, the answer is no. This is not your fault. Either of you. It is entirely down to me and is not because of anything either of you have done. It is something inside me which I cannot control and cannot deal with.

If nasty things are said about me, please don't feel bad for me. I probably deserve them. In any case, I tried my best. I always tried my best. For both of you. Everything I ever did was with the best interests of both of you at heart. Sometimes, I will have failed. Sometimes I will have misjudged the situation and done the wrong thing. But please know that my intentions were always good. Everything I did was for you.

Chris, I'm so sorry for what I did to you. I can't excuse it — I can barely explain it — but please know that I'm sorry. I hope you are able to find peace. It will hurt at first. You might feel guilty. But don't. This is the only way it could ever have ended, no matter what we did. I hope one day you are able to accept that. It might take a while for the fog to clear and for you to be able to see things from the other side, but time is a great healer. I know that with time you will find peace with what happened. And I know you will look after Evie.

Evie, you might never read this and you almost certainly won't remember me. You'll have photos, no doubt, but you won't remember the sound of my voice or the smell of my perfume. All you'll have is what other people tell you about me. No memories of your own. For that, please know that I am eternally sorry. It might help you in the long run. I can only imagine you might miss me less for never knowing me, but please know that I will always miss you more than you will ever know. When you have children of your own, you will come to understand what I mean. I hope you can forgive me. This is not what I wanted, but it is how it has to be.

Please know that I was not a bad person. Things were different before I got ill. I can blame no-one but myself for what happened. You might wonder if I could have got better with help. If something could have been done to stop this happening. The answer to both of those questions is no.

I can see things clearly now. This was not an act of despera-

tion or a cry for help. I was not in a confused state. For the first time in a long time, I was able to see things for what they really were. Please know that I went in peace, with full clarity of mind and with the best of intentions. Please know that this was what I wanted.

All that is left for me to say is that I am sorry for everything. I hope you remember me fondly and that all the bad things that happened can be forgiven, if not forgotten. I never meant for any of it to happen, and I hope that you are able to move on with your lives now that I am gone. I'm safe now. Everyone is safe now.

I will be looking down on you always. I will watch out for you and guide you where you need guidance. Now I have no pain. Now I have no other calling, no other role than to love you. I will be there. I love you both more than you will ever know.

Mummy

xxx

FORTY-NINE

MEGAN. TWO DAYS LATER

The first thing I hear is the sound of my own breath, shallow and rattling. My whole body tingles, a kaleidoscope of colours plays out across my mind. The pain almost splits my head in two. My jaw hurts, but I can't move it. There's something in my mouth, holding it open. I open my mouth ever so slightly more. It can't open much further, but it clicks and snaps as it moves, as if my jaw hasn't moved for days.

Slowly, I try to open my eyes. The light burns at first, searing the backs of my eyeballs like a roaring hot flame. I hear bleeping, and the faint sound of a television on the other side of the room. I recognise the programme as *Bargain Hunt* before I realise where I am and what's going on.

I move my right hand out to the side and feel the metal frame of the bed rising up, keeping me in. I roll my head to the left, feeling and hearing my neck cricking and cracking as it moves. I hear someone stand up and rush out of the room, leaving a breeze of cold air that sweeps across my chest and face.

Moments later, I hear the door open again.

'How long ago?' a male voice says.

'Literally just now. I came straight out,' says a female voice — one I recognise.

The man speaks again. 'It's okay, Megan. You lie back and relax. I'm just going to check a couple of things and we'll be right with you.'

I hear him pressing buttons next to me.

'Is everything okay?' the woman asks.

'Seems to be fine. Can you hear me, Megan?'

I try to say yes, but the thing in my mouth stops me from saying anything. I nod my head, but I don't know if they see it. My skull feels so heavy, as if it's been filled with concrete.

'You're in hospital, Megan. Nothing to worry about. We're looking after you just fine. My name's Mr Grilby. I'm the senior consultant here. Do you have any pain anywhere? You can point, if that helps.'

Slowly, I point to my head, and to my jaw.

'The headache's understandable. Is the pain in your jaw because of the breathing apparatus?'

So that's what it is. I nod my head slowly.

'I see. I'm just going to have a listen to your breathing, if that's okay. My stethoscope might be a little cold.' He goes quiet for a couple of seconds before I feel the stethoscope on my chest. 'The fluid seems to be clearing very nicely, actually. Shall we have a go at sitting you up slowly and seeing how you get on with the finest natural air the city has to offer?'

I groan something that's meant to sound like 'Yes please', and my bed begins to rise, accompanied by an electronic whirring.

'Let me know if anything hurts, Megan. You might feel a little stiff.' Understatement of the century, that. 'Okay. Now I'm just going to take this out of your mouth. You might cough a little, but don't worry. I'll take your hand. If you struggle to catch your breath, just squeeze and I'll pop this straight back in, alright?'

I nod, and he takes the piece of plastic out of my mouth.

He's right — I do start to cough, and it feels as though my lungs are on fire. It's almost as if it's clearing them out, and I battle through, desperate not to squeeze his hand. A few seconds later, I catch my breath, look at him and nod.

'Good. Good. Don't worry if you feel a little woozy. That was quite some sleep. Even my fourteen-year-old would be pushed to compete with you on that front. Just so you know and don't get alarmed, you've got a couple of cannulas in your hand, here. They've been feeding and watering you while you've been snoozing. Much better than trying to cook dinner, eh?'

I can't say I agree with him, but I appreciate his attempts at light-hearted humour.

'Right. I'll get a nurse in to keep an eye on you and to

do a couple of post-wakeywakey checks. I'll leave you with her for a few moments. Shout if you need anything,' he says, but not to me.

The door closes behind him and it's just the two of us left in the room.

I roll my head to the side and look at Lauren. I can't quite decipher the look on her face. It seems to show every emotion rolled into one. Lauren's not usually the sort of person to show any emotion at all, so it surprises me a little.

'What are you doing here?' I ask, my voice like sandpaper on a chalkboard.

'Looking after you,' she says. 'Chris was in earlier. Now it's my turn. Mum's popping in this evening.'

'How long?' I say, trying to keep the words to a minimum.

'In here? Two days so far. They'll want to keep you in for further observation. They'll probably want to have a chat with you, too.'

The meaning of what she says is clear to me. The doctors will want me to speak to a counsellor or psychologist of some sort.

Lauren's silent for a good thirty seconds or so before she speaks again. There's a sharp pain in my abdomen, which I presume is from the stomach pumping.

'I was at Mum's for a bit when she was looking after Evie. I didn't know she was going to be there, I promise. Mum tried calling you to see when you wanted to pick her up, but you didn't answer. She called Chris but his mobile was off, so we went over to the house with Mum's key and let ourselves in. I went through to the kitchen first.'

The blood.

'Don't worry. Mum didn't see anything. The police knocked at the door a few seconds after we got in, to say a dog walker had found you in the stream and recognised you. They said you were unconscious but alive. I took the note. Mum hasn't seen it. No-one's seen it.'

I ask her with my eyes whether she read it. She avoids my gaze, and I know I have my answer.

'I don't know how cryptic you were trying to be, but I read between the lines,' she says, not making eye contact with me. 'It's now a small pile of ashes in my fireplace.'

I'm unsure how to respond to this. What does she mean when she says she read between the lines? A large part of me doesn't want to know.

'I haven't told anyone about the note,' she says, her voice lowered. 'As far as I'm concerned, no-one needs to know. And I thought you should know that things are completely finished with Chris, too. That won't be happening again. I know it doesn't change what happened in the past, but I thought it was important that you knew.'

I really don't know what to make of what she's saying. Is this some sort of power play? A case of 'I know something about you that no-one else does'? I wouldn't put it past her. I say nothing in return.

'Listen, Megan, I'm sorry. I'm so, so sorry for what

happened.' I hear her voice cracking, and in that moment I know she's being truthful. 'I never meant for any of it. We've all just been so... distant. Life got in the way, and we let it. I can't change what happened, and I know you might never be able to forgive me, but I just wanted you to know that I'm sorry.'

Before I can say anything, the pain in my stomach returns again, this time building in a crescendo of agony. I can't catch my breath. I start to see black spots and stars around the edges of my vision. I roll onto my side to try and stem the pain, but I can't.

It won't go.

Won't go.

FIFTY

CHRIS. ONE YEAR LATER

I pause as I walk past the microwave and catch sight of the time. 16:42. Exactly one year. To the minute.

The past year has been a rollercoaster of emotion. Watching Evie grow up more quickly than I could ever have imagined, and doing it all without her mum. Sometimes I sit and watch her sleeping, wondering how on earth such a tiny brain can process everything that's happened. She seems beautifully oblivious to most of it. I hope she is, anyway.

After pausing for a moment, I realise I need to occupy my mind. I sit at the kitchen table and sort through the post that arrived this morning. There's a bill for the new soffits, gutters and fascias I had replaced when we moved into the new house. The old ones were wooden and rotten, and desperately needed replacing. The new house is smaller than the old one, so there was some money left over for a few renovations. There's also a letter I've been waiting for for a long time. That it should arrive today is either a blessing or an insult.

I open it, scanning my eyes down past the NHS logo and letterhead, before reading the content of the letter itself.

In short, it's a grovelling apology. They've agreed to settle out of court for their failings a year ago. The sum is substantial, but I won't see a penny of it. I'll be putting it straight into a trust fund for Evie. A nest egg for when she's older. A legacy from her mum.

There's still no explanation as to how it happened. There's no paragraph telling us how they managed to not even suspect gastrointestinal perforation in a patient who'd taken a massive drug overdose, nor how they failed to notice the symptoms in time to avoid the development of peritonitis — the lone, empty word that was eventually written in brackets on her death certificate, right next to 'multiple organ failure'.

It's a word devoid of all meaning. Her whole life ended by a fuck-up, a word that can only be expanded upon by reaching for the dictionary. Even then, *Inflammation of the peritoneum, typically caused by bacterial infection either via the blood or after rupture of an abdominal organ* is hardly a fitting description for the agonising death she had to endure.

The most painful thing for me is that I don't know if that was what she wanted. Only two days earlier she had tried to end her own life. Was she thankful when she woke up in the hospital bed that day, or was she disappointed that her attempts had failed? Was she happy when she finally realised she was dying? She would have been in an incredible amount of pain, that much we know. That's what makes it harder. If she'd gone relatively peacefully under her own terms, that would have been much easier to take.

I don't know what I'll tell Evie. One day she's going to ask. She'll want to know what happened. And I really don't know what I'm going to say.

It would be fair to say I feel guilty. Of course I do. Megan would never have attempted to end her own life if I hadn't had an affair. I knew my actions could potentially devastate the family, but I never saw this coming in a million years. How am I going to explain that to Evie?

These are all things I need to get straight in my head sooner or later. She's already an inquisitive little child, and that's not going to stop any time soon. It's only a matter of time before she starts asking the difficult questions, and there's no-one else I can palm her off onto.

Megan's family have been a tower of strength. Even Lauren seems to have been changed by what happened. Part of me wonders whether she feels guilty too. She certainly seems to be under some sort of emotional burden. Maybe one day she'll be able to free herself of it.

I don't know if it was Megan's death that did it, but she and James decided they were going to try and put everything behind them and move forward together. I hope for their sake that they can. James barely speaks to me, but that's understandable. In time, we'll be able to move on. There is more that unites us than divides us, especially after the events of a year ago. Evie's growing up fast, and I'm pleased at how we are able to come together for her. The poor little mite's lost more than she knows, and there's not one of us that's going to do anything other than give her all the love in the world.

The village held a memorial service for Riley and Kai recently, between the first anniversaries of their deaths. The police took the opportunity to make a statement about the crimes still being unsolved — a completely pointless exercise which did nothing but stir up the local sense of anger which had since subsided. I'm sure they were trying to be helpful and remind the public that they still needed their help, but people round here have long since given up on that idea.

A week after Megan passed away, news broke that an old fella had died in the next village. Turns out he'd been a convicted sex offender with a string of crimes committed against children. There was nothing to link him to Riley and Kai — the police said as much themselves — but the guy had originally asked to be housed in our village. It was only the fact that it would have put him within a couple of hundred yards of a primary school which meant the authorities rejected the request and housed him in the next village instead. Perhaps it was just a coincidence. But as far as people round here are concerned, he is the most likely candidate. Now that he's dead and buried, we'll never know.

I flick the switch on the kettle just as Evie comes

toddling into the kitchen, holding her toy rabbit by its long, floppy ear.

'Daddy, not working,' she says, with a pout I definitely recognise but haven't seen in at least a year.

'What's not working? The TV?'

She nods.

'Alright, sweetie. I'll come through and fix it in a minute. I'm just making a cup of tea.'

'No, now,' she says, as she screws up her face and forces a tear to run down her cheek.

I scoop her up in my arms and rub her back as she cries on my shoulder.

'Are you tired?'

'No,' she says, rubbing her eyes and yawning.

'Alright. Shall we sit and watch TV together? Have a cuddle?'

She nods, so I finish making my tea before we head through to the living room.

I start to tune out the excitable sounds and flashing colours on the screen as I feel the warmth of Evie sitting across my lap, her head resting on my chest as she sucks her thumb.

In moments like this, I'm happy. I can forget everything, if only for a minute or two. When the fog has temporarily lifted, I can see further. The horizon seems brighter. And that's when I know.

We'll be alright.

GET MORE OF MY BOOKS FREE!

Thank you for reading *Tell Me I'm Wrong*. I hope it was as much fun for you as it was for me writing it.

To say thank you, I'd like to invite you to my exclusive *VIP Club*, and give you some of my books and short stories for FREE. All members of my VIP Club have access to FREE, exclusive books and short stories which aren't available anywhere else.

You'll also get access to all of my new releases at a bargain-basement price before they're available anywhere else. Joining is absolutely FREE and you can leave at any time, no questions asked. To join the club, head to adamcroft.net/vip-club **and two free books will be sent to you straight away!**

If you enjoyed the book, please do leave a review on the site you bought it from. Reviews mean an awful lot to writers and they help us to find new readers more than almost anything else. It would be very much appreciated.

I love hearing from my readers, too, so please do feel free to get in touch with me. You can contact me via my website, on Twitter @adamcroft and you can 'like' my Facebook page at facebook.com/adamcroftbooks.

For more information, visit my website: adamcroft.net

CLOSER TO YOU

What if your loved one wanted you dead?

Grace wants to spend the rest of her life with Tom. She needs to. Because otherwise he'll kill her.

He's the perfect gentleman. He's kind, attentive and caring. Her family love him. And he needs Grace dead. But why

As the feeling grows that Tom is not as perfect as he seems, he begins to slowly and systematically destroy her life. Can she discover the truth and escape with her life?

Visit adamcroft.net/book/closer-to-you/ to grab your copy.

THE PERFECT LIE

What if you were framed for a murder you didn't commit?

Amy Walker lives the perfect family life with her husband and two young sons. Until a knock at the door turns their lives upside down.

It's the police. Her father-in-law is dead and they're arresting her for his murder.

The evidence against her is overwhelming. Forensics and witnesses place her at the scene. But there's only one problem:

She didn't do it.

With her family destroyed and a murder sentence looming, Amy must discover who murdered her father-in-law — and why they're so hell-bent on framing her as the killer.

Visit adamcroft.net/book/the-perfect-lie/ to grab your copy.

IN HER IMAGE

Alice Jefferson has a new friend. He wants her dead.

He's been in her house while she's been sleeping. He follows her every time she leaves the house. She knows exactly who he is.

The police can find no trace of him having ever existed.

And then she uncovers a shocking secret that turns her entire world upside down, and leaves her unable to trust anybody — even herself.

HER LAST TOMORROW

Could you murder your wife to save your daughter?

On the surface, Nick Connor's life is seemingly perfect: a quiet life with his beautiful family and everything he could ever want. But soon his murky past will collide with his idyllic life and threaten the very people he loves the most in the world.

When his five-year-old daughter, Ellie, is kidnapped, Nick's life is thrown into a tailspin. In exchange for his daughter's safe return, Nick will have to do the unthinkable: **he must murder his wife**.

With his family's lives hanging in the balance, what will Nick do? Can he and his family survive when the evil that taunts them stems from the sins of his past?

Visit adamcroft.net/book/her-last-tomorrow/ to grab your copy.

ONLY THE TRUTH

He's not the perfect husband. But he is the perfect suspect.

Dan Cooper has never been the perfect husband to Lisa. He travels for work and plays the carefree bachelor when he can. But now, on a solo business trip, in a remote coastal hotel, he's surprised to find Lisa in his bathroom. She's dead.

He has no idea how she got there but one chilling fact is clear: everything points to Dan having murdered her. Someone is trying to frame him. Someone who might still be watching. In a panic, he goes on the run. But even as he flees across Europe, his unknown enemy stacks up the evidence against him.

Dan is determined to clear his name and take revenge on Lisa's killer, but the culprit is closing in. And then there's the agony of his own guilty conscience. No, he didn't kill her—but is it all his fault?

Visit adamcroft.net/book/only-the-truth/ to grab your copy.